I0542066

Totally Five Star: New Delhi

KISMET

JASMINE HILL

Kismet
ISBN # 978-1-78651-941-2
©Copyright Jasmine Hill 2016
Cover Art by Posh Gosh ©Copyright April 2016
Interior text design by Claire Siemaszkiewicz
Totally Bound Publishing

KISMET

Dedication

To my dear friend, Daphne Chauhan — thank you so much for your assistance! I miss the good times we shared in India…

Chapter One

Tanvi took a deep breath and inhaled the sweet, floral scent of the many flowers crowded into the garden beds. Peacocks strutted around the grounds, the lone male's tail feathers splayed proudly, showing off the beautiful green and turquoise plumes in his standard courtship ritual.

She was sitting in her usual spot, under a shade canopy provided by an Indian rosewood. It was her custom before her weekly meeting with George Benson, the Totally Five Star New Delhi Finance Manager. She loved coming to the hotel. It was like an oasis in the desert, providing her with much-needed respite from the sweaty heat and bodies of the city. A large kidney-shaped pond provided a tranquil vista. Fat gold and white koi drifted lazily, hiding under the water lilies then darting out to gulp down unsuspecting insects. The beautiful garden was her sanctuary, a peaceful haven that she used to think. She gazed around at the few hotel guests also taking refuge in the serenity, some reading, others just sitting and relaxing. She always allowed herself half an hour in the koi garden. It was enough time to recharge her batteries and shake off the grime of the city.

Tanvi looked at her watch, sighed and rose to her feet. She strode into the magnificent Totally Five Star foyer and took a moment to appreciate her surroundings. The air conditioning immediately provided a cool, crisp reprieve from the cloyingly hot outside temperature. Large bamboo ceiling fans rotated slowly, dispersing the cool air. Patchouli incense burned discreetly in brass burners spotted around the vast lobby. Large, ornate wall hangings of peacocks adorned the white walls. She'd determined some time ago that when she finally moved out of the suffocating environment of her family home, she was going to invest in one of the elaborate embroideries for herself. They were true works of art, particularly when one imagined the hard-working ladies of Rajasthan hunched over the black velvet fabric, needles strung with rich thread as they hand-sewed the birds in beautiful detail.

Handmade red and blue silk rugs lay scattered across the marble floors, giving a traditional look and feel. She glanced to her right and ran her hand admiringly across the highly polished surface of the sheesham wood side table. She loved the fact that the Totally Five Star had contracted Indian craftsmen to make all their furniture but had also ensured that the wood had been sustainably sourced. The grand foyer was dotted with lovely Indian-inspired sheesham furnishings, adding a decidedly authentic impression. She loved it.

She took a seat on one of the cotton-upholstered armchairs. Again, she'd been impressed by the hotel's support of local employment and skill. They'd commissioned a not-for-profit organization to create the fabric using the traditional block printing technique. She smoothed a hand across the lush fabric and imagined the ladies hand-stamping the cotton in the traditional Rajasthan way. She looked at her watch again. George was running late. They generally met in the foyer first then decided if they would move to George's office or the lobby restaurant. Tanvi hoped he'd opt for the restaurant. It overlooked the lovely grounds and she preferred it to George's chaotic office.

She heard his telltale English accent and looked up. He was striding across the lobby, a pile of paperwork in one hand and a mobile in the other. His ruddy complexion was even redder today and he was breathing heavily, the Indian heat obviously getting to him. When he saw her, he broke into his usual good-natured smile. He hung up his mobile and tossed his paperwork on a nearby chair.

"Tanvi, my dear. How are you?"

Tanvi rose and smiled at the affable Englishman. She liked George and seeing him always made her day brighter. "George, I'm well." She grasped his outstretched hand and indicated his paperwork with a nod. "I see we have some work ahead of us."

He chuckled. "It's not as bad as it looks, I assure you. Just some taxation matters to go over."

"Shall we sit in the restaurant?" Tanvi proposed. "I could really use a cup of tea and one of your divine pastries."

George gathered up his paperwork. "Of course. I could use a change of scenery. I've been dealing with payroll all morning."

Tanvi looked at him in surprise. "Where's your assistant?"

"Isha had some family matter to attend to." He shrugged then chuckled. "She'll be back soon and it's good for me to get my hand in every now and again. I get rusty with the processes otherwise. It just means that I'm incredibly busy. I would have canceled our meeting this morning, but I need to go over these issues with you."

"Are you sure you can take the time? I can come back when Isha has returned. Surely the tax can wait a few days?"

George winked at her. "Not at all, and besides, I too am looking forward to one of our fabulous pastries." He rubbed his substantial belly. "Although my wife would have my head if she knew. She has me on a strict diet." He gave a heavy sigh. "Cholesterol."

They'd entered the lobby restaurant where the hotel guests were finishing their breakfasts. Tanvi gazed at the delicious spread of food—exotic fruit, yogurt, pastries and the famous South Indian pancakes, *dosas*, served with every imaginable accompaniment.

They found a vacant table by the window overlooking the koi garden. Tanvi glanced at the pile of paperwork in George's arms, an idea popping into her head. She could fill in for Isha. It would give her some time out of the office and a much-needed change. She mentally checked her schedule. There was nothing urgent and she knew her father would approve of the idea—the Totally Five Star was one of their best clients, after all.

"George, why don't I fill in for Isha? I have nothing that can't wait and you look like you could use the help."

George scratched his chin in thought. "It would help me out tremendously. Would your father mind?"

Tanvi smiled. "I'm sure he would be more than happy for me to assist. I'll call him when we've concluded our meeting."

* * * *

Alexander gazed around the busy Indira Gandhi International Airport. His usual driver, Sanjay, should be waiting for him. Finally, he spotted the little man bouncing around and waving his arms in the air, trying to be seen behind a group of other people. Alexander saw Sanjay easily — Alex's height raised him above most of the locals.

"Mr. Alex. Boss," Sanjay cried, his voice high with excitement and breaking through the din.

Alexander strode toward him, elbowing his way through the crowd. He'd visited India enough times now to appreciate that the only way to get anywhere was via a somewhat aggressive approach — after all, when in Rome...

He made it through the cluster of bodies and presented himself to Sanjay.

"Boss! You made it. Good flight?" Sanjay grabbed Alex's suitcase and, ignoring the wheels, started dragging it toward the exit. Alexander winced as his Tumi luggage was unceremoniously hauled over the dirty airport floor.

"Yes, a good flight. Thank you, Sanjay. Here, let me." Alex relieved the little man of the weighty case. "Why don't you take this one?" He thrust his smaller onboard bag at the driver.

Sanjay grinned happily and started once more for the doors. As they walked through the exit, immediately the oppressive Delhi heat hit Alexander. It took his breath away for a moment and he had to stop in his tracks, the air burning his lungs. The smell of the city struck him next, a smell that he always detected when he first arrived but that seemed to disappear after a few minutes, probably because he adjusted to it. It wasn't bad particularly, just — different.

Sanjay stopped by a black SUV. A good choice, Alex noted. He always paid Sanjay extra to hire a decent car, as he couldn't abide traveling around the hot and chaotic streets without air-conditioned comfort. Sanjay had parked not far from the entrance with the two front wheels on the walkway, the back end jutting out precariously into the road. Alexander shook his head and placed his luggage in the trunk. It always amazed him how the local people parked anywhere and everywhere. However, he'd be willing to bet that the airport's parking rules were stricter than elsewhere. Sanjay was lucky not to have been given a fine.

Alexander stepped into the back of the car and they took off, Sanjay providing a continuous commentary of events since Alex's last visit. The traffic was standard and they made reasonable time. Again, it never ceased to amaze him that, even though the traffic was heavy and rules appeared to be for guidance only, cars actually moved. Of course drivers had to be aggressive to get anywhere, but rarely had Alex encountered a traffic gridlock like what was common in Sydney and London.

Soon they were pulling up in front of the Totally Five Star New Delhi. A porter opened Alexander's door and another retrieved his luggage, instigating a comical tug of war with Sanjay.

Alexander rescued his baggage from Sanjay's eager clutches and made quick arrangements with him for the following morning. He handed the suitcase to the waiting porter along with some rupee notes for a tip and strode up the marble steps to the terrace. Two enormous potted ferns stood either side of the wide stairway, their leafy fronds impressing upon guests a cool freshness. Marble elephants, trunks raised to the heavens, stood guard at either side of the automated glass doors and huge bamboo ceiling fans whirred above.

It was Alex's third stay at the Totally Five Star New Delhi. Whenever he could, wherever he was in the world, he always booked into the Totally Five Star. They were different in every city and that was part of the charm. Here in New Delhi, the hotel was a modern building, built for purpose. The architecture was contemporary and designed to wear well in the harsh environment.

A security checkpoint, standard in all good Indian hotels, was positioned to the left of the doors with an X-ray machine and, beside it, a metal detector and two security guards standing nearby. Alex placed his briefcase on the conveyer belt and started to empty his pockets.

One of the security guards stepped forward. "It is okay, sir," he said and motioned for Alexander to go around the metal detector.

"But I have metal in my pockets," Alex told him, jiggling his change.

"Yes, I know. But we check your briefcase."

Alex chuckled to himself. He'd forgotten about this amusing little quirk of the Indian security. Apparently only his briefcase was of interest, or perhaps it was because he looked like an honest guy. Who knew? He recalled an incident on his previous visit, when he'd purchased a box of wine from one of the shopping malls. When he'd arrived at the security point, the guard had helpfully held Alex's box of wine while he walked through the metal detector, then he had handed it back to Alex once he was on the other side, the box of wine going completely unchecked. It was just one of the many things he enjoyed about India.

He entered through the doors into the cool interior and breathed a sigh of relief. Two women waited for him inside the entrance. One, he recalled, was the guest liaison officer, her name badge reading Hannah. She stepped forward, her brightly colored saree swishing as she moved.

"Welcome back, Mr. Banks. Namaste," she greeted him with her palms placed together.

Alex returned the traditional greeting as the other woman placed a spot of ochre-colored powder between his eyes.

"Please, come this way," Hannah requested.

Alex followed her to a cozy alcove. A jug of cold water with cucumber and orange slices sat on a low wooden table, a platter filled with Indian sweets sitting next to it.

Hannah handed him some paperwork. "I have your check-in information here. Please ensure we have the details correct. We have you booked into one of our suites as you requested. It's ready for you. I'll have the porters take your luggage up."

Alexander scanned the paperwork and poured himself a glass of water, the cool, lightly scented liquid soothing his parched throat. He signed the documents where necessary and passed them over. "Thank you, Hannah."

She blushed at the use of her name. "Is there anything else you need, Mr. Banks? Do you recall all the facilities and services we offer?"

He remembered their facilities perfectly. He'd used their state-of-the-art gym every morning, had experienced an Indian therapeutic massage when his shoulders had been particularly tight, had swum in one of their three pools every day and had dined in their Indian restaurant, which was rated number one in the country. He was aware they offered a host of other services, but was yet to use any of them, his stay always being related to business and not pleasure.

"I do, thank you. I think I'll just head up to my suite."

"Of course. Your valet is Deepak. He'll be with you for your entire stay." Hannah motioned to a man standing nearby attired in black trousers and a white dress shirt.

"Mr. Banks, sir, I will show you to your rooms."

Alexander stood and followed Deepak to the elevator bank. The scent of incense wafting around the lobby gave him a sudden sense of déjà vu and took him back to his last visit at the hotel.

The elevator arrived and Alexander stepped in, followed by Deepak who proceeded to talk him through the security processes.

His suite was located on the twentieth floor. Deepak opened the door and ushered him in. Alex studied the rooms. He didn't know anything about interior design but he liked what the decorator had done with the suite. The furniture, modern and in neutral shades in order not to detract from the colorful Indian artwork, was comfortable and elegant. A six-seated dining table took up most of the dining area and a sectional lounge, upholstered in a tan fabric, provided a comfortable sitting area. An Indian wood cabinet hid the large flat-screen TV and dark teak side tables stood at either end of the sectional sofa. White muslin curtains hung at the large windows. Indian cotton and silk rugs in deep blues and reds lay scattered across the tiled floor.

A kitchenette was located off the dining area. Alex recalled from his last visit that the valets would also cook for him, if he required it.

"I will unpack your bags, Mr. Alex. Can I get you anything?"

He hadn't eaten in a while, preferring to sleep on the plane. "Perhaps a sandwich. I'll retrieve my toiletries and a change of clothes before you unpack. I need a shower."

Alexander strode into the bedroom and rummaged in his luggage for what he needed. He located his small personal bag. It contained sex toys that he was sure would send poor Deepak into heart palpitations. It was one of his *things* — whenever he traveled, he always packed a selection. He wasn't sure what to expect or who to expect it with, but he had a number of women friends across the globe and one in particular who would often take time out of her modeling schedule to make a side trip. He was a man with needs, and hard fucking was the best way he knew to blow off steam after a particularly challenging business meeting.

He studied the king-size bed. It definitely had potential. The brass rungs on the headboard would be perfect to tie a woman up to. A white cotton bedspread covered the mattress and a mosquito net hung from the ceiling, enveloping the bed. It was a little whimsical for his tastes, but the ladies would love it.

Alex took his toiletries into the adjoining bathroom. It was spacious and tiled in white marble, a clawfoot tub sat under the window and a large shower recess took up an entire corner. Double sinks were on the right-hand wall, a selection of Indian aromatherapy products in a basket to the side. It was his kind of bathroom, unfussy and classy.

He was looking forward to washing the grime of the trip off his body, then he'd have a sandwich and a beer and an early night.

Chapter Two

Alexander was reviewing some paperwork in readiness for his first meeting of the morning. He could have had breakfast in his suite, but he wanted to get out among people and he was meeting the Totally Five Star manager for coffee. He and Jay had attended school together, Jay's Indian-Australian parents having remained in Australia while Jay had decided to move to New Delhi and take up the managerial position at the hotel.

Alex looked up to scan the restaurant for his friend and his eyes locked on a woman across the room. His breath hitched and his gaze drank her in. She was stunning! Her ebony hair hung in a thick braid down her back, the tip brushing the top of her lush ass as she sashayed across the room. The emerald saree she wore was tied low on her hips, accentuating their sway and giving him a glimpse of a taut abdomen. His gaze traveled up to meet her face and he sucked in a breath when she stared at him. Her hazel-green eyes were slightly almond in shape, her cheekbones high and defined, giving her an exotic beauty. She'd piled fruit on a plate and was heading toward him on her way back to her table. His cock grew solid as he stared at her, unable to drag his gaze away. Her caramel skin emphasized the green of her eyes so they seemed to bore straight through him as she passed in a swish of soft material and a waft of floral.

"That's Tanvi Sharma," a deep voice said from beside him.

Alex startled and turned his gaze on his friend.

Jay chuckled and shook his head. "You're not the first man to be dazzled by her. She's quite beautiful."

Alex stood and thrust a hand out to Jay. "Good to see you."

"And you. I trust that everything is to your liking?"

"Of course." Alex pulled out a chair and indicated for his friend to join him.

Jay called over a waiter and proceeded to order pastries and coffee, and Alex took the opportunity to study the woman once more. She'd joined a friend at a nearby table, both of them giggling over something.

"What brings you to New Delhi this time, Alex?"

Alexander turned his attention to Jay. "I'm looking at investing in a small, local IT company. They have some innovative ideas but don't have the funding to take them further. They want a silent investor, someone prepared to take a step back and let them run with what they have." He shrugged. "It's early days yet. I still have a lot more business analysis to conduct. I have some of my main people arriving in a week to review the company's initial proposal and discuss things further. Of course, there are strict FDI rules that my lawyers are looking at now, and—how do I say this delicately? — the Indian people can be a little...challenging to work with. I have to ensure that this business investment will be to both of our benefits."

Jay nodded. "Why have they approached you to be a silent investor?"

Alexander shrugged. "Perhaps out of sight means out of mind. Depending on the amount I'm going to invest, I'll establish one of my people here as liaison to ensure that everything is operating aboveboard." Alex gave him a level look. "And that there is no, shall we say, misappropriation of funds."

Jay smiled. "That would be very wise."

"So how do you know her?" Alex asked, nodding his head in the direction of Tanvi's table.

"Her father's firm is contracted to us to provide financial services. Tanvi's a tax accountant. She's usually here once a week, but she's assisting George, our finance manager, while his assistant is away."

Alex leaned back in his chair and studied the woman thoughtfully. Perhaps this dull business trip was looking up. He was determined to get to know Tanvi Sharma. He could already imagine tying her up to his bed and having his wicked way with her. He envisioned smoothing a leather riding crop over her flawless caramel skin and bringing it down across that lush, round ass.

He shifted in his seat, his cock pressing painfully against his dress pants. Christ, he had to get a grip or he'd embarrass himself.

He glanced across the table to where Jay was smirking at him. "What?"

His friend laughed and shook his head. "I know what you're thinking, Alex and I don't believe that Tanvi

Sharma will be as easy to charm as your usual conquests."

Challenge accepted, Jay, my friend. Bring it on!

Tanvi gazed across the restaurant to where the gentleman sat with the Totally Five Star manager. She wasn't oblivious to his interest. She'd stared straight at him when he'd appeared to be undressing her with his eyes and it had taken all of her self-control to appear composed and unaffected.

"He is sooo hot!" Riya loud-whispered, fanning her face theatrically. "And he's obviously into you."

Tanvi glared at her friend. "Will you keep your voice down!"

In truth, Tanvi couldn't understand why the man seemed so interested in her, particularly when she was sitting with Riya, who looked amazing in wide-legged, navy linen pants cinched tight at the waist and a white silk blouse.

She surreptitiously studied the man from under lowered lashes as she picked at the fruit on her plate. He was really attractive. He definitely took care of himself and she imagined he'd be using the hotel's gym facilities on a daily basis. Even under his blue dress shirt she could see the definition in his arms and chest and, when he moved, his shirt strained slightly around his broad shoulders. When she'd looked directly at him on her way back from the breakfast buffet, she'd immediately noticed his blue eyes, piercing ice-blue, which were slightly intimidating. He had a scar dissecting his right cheek but, rather than marring what could have been considered a beautiful face it gave him a sexy and dangerous edge. She'd barely been able to contain her shudder of awareness as she'd walked by him. She took another quick peek across at him and decided that he swam a lot—his muscular shoulders and sun-streaked brown hair indicated that he spent time outside and in the water.

Tanvi glanced across at Riya, who was ogling the man blatantly. "Look at that hard jaw!" she whispered. "He just seems so…so *masculine*."

Tanvi rolled her eyes. "You've been watching too many Hollywood movies."

"Well, that man could have stepped directly out of a movie set where he's the sexy, brooding hero," Riya breathed with exaggerated awe. "He has alpha male written all over him."

Tanvi laughed. "And what do you know about alpha males?"

"What don't I know? You're aware that I'm hardly a blushing maiden." She smirked. "And I've read quite a bit of erotica and, you know, we have some good erotic authors here in India."

Tanvi shook her head, intrigued. She didn't know of any Indian erotic novelists.

"Oh yes," Riya continued, dropping her head closer to Tanvi's. "I've just finished a book called *Panty*, by Sangeeta Bandyopadhyay." She gave Tanvi a curious look. "You have read *Fifty Shades of Grey*, haven't you?"

"I have," Tanvi admitted. What she wasn't going to admit to Riya was how intrigued she'd become when she'd read about the BDSM aspects in the book. It had pulled a fierce desire from deep in her belly where so far there'd only been a void. She'd read every BDSM story she could get her hands on once she'd realized that the subject could ignite a fire in her psyche. Perhaps it was a form of self-torture and maybe she was a masochist, because kismet had ordained that there would be no dreamy, dominant male in her future.

Riya eyed her pointedly. "Well, you know what I'm talking about when I describe a man as an alpha male."

"Well, yes. I guess I do. Have you seen the movie?"

"No," Riya scoffed. "But it's the first thing I'm going to do when I visit my cousin in England next month."

Tanvi continually marveled at her friend's willingness to thumb her nose at conventions. Riya was always outraged at the Indian censorship and what she considered the stuffy conservatism of society. She traveled to England once a year to visit with family there, and she always returned with new ideas and talk of her risky adventures. Tanvi had to agree with her. Tanvi's few years at college in America had opened her eyes to a modern, much less conservative way of thinking. When she was studying there, it was the first time in her life that she'd felt free to do what she wanted without fear of censure or recrimination.

"You know…" Riya tapped her finger on the table for emphasis. "You'd understand exactly what to look for in an alpha male if you'd read some more erotic novels, Tanvi. I can give you some titles to try."

Tanvi sighed. "I'm not completely oblivious. I know men."

Riya rolled her eyes. "But not the right ones. You haven't exactly had a good track record."

"I haven't been scraping the bottom of the barrel, either," Tanvi snapped.

"No, they've been very…appropriate. Wealthy and considered good matches by your family, but did you ever feel any passion?"

Tanvi looked at her watch, suddenly irritated with her friend. "Thanks for breakfast but I have to go. George and I have a lot to get through today."

Riya stood with her. "Will I see you at yoga later?"

"Perhaps," Tanvi responded noncommittally. She gave Riya a quick kiss on the cheek and picked up her handbag. "Have a good day."

She turned to walk away then stopped abruptly, unwilling to leave her friend on such terse terms. She faced Riya once again. "I've wanted to try the yoga class offered here at the hotel. Why don't you join me? It starts at six p.m."

Riya smiled brightly. "That sounds fantastic. I'll see you then." She winked, grabbed her bag and sauntered off toward the restaurant exit.

Tanvi recommenced making her way to the hotel administration offices. She shouldn't have been short with Riya. Her friend was just pointing things out as she saw them, but Riya was right and had hit a raw nerve. Tanvi had never felt any passion in any of her few relationships. In fact, she wasn't even sure what the word meant and, sadly, her life appeared closer to leading her in a direction where she'd never discover this phantom emotion.

She reached Isha's desk, sat and logged on with the password that George had organized for her. As the computer booted up, she thought back to her conversation with Riya. Tanvi had read many romances, but she'd given up on the pastime when it had started to feel like a form of self-flagellation. She hadn't wanted to see the look of sympathy in Riya's eyes she would have prompted by admitting that fact. But seeing that gentleman at breakfast had stirred something deep in Tanvi's belly—a girl had to have someone to fantasize about, after all.

Tanvi's life was sorely lacking in anyone remotely intense or sexual. Maybe it was time to drag out those novels.

Chapter Three

Alexander looked at his watch — three p.m. He'd had a slow day of trawling through paperwork. He should leave all of this tedious work to his team, but he'd wanted to get a head start and he required a reasonable perspective on where things stood within the company before the others arrived. He rubbed his forehead. It was time to take a break. Perhaps he'd call it quits for the day and head back to the Totally Five Star for a workout and a swim. He needed the release that exercise always brought him.

He leaned back in his chair and stared out at the chaotic street, his thoughts drifting inexplicably to the exotic creature he'd seen in the restaurant that morning. He'd been able to push her to the back of his mind while he'd been occupied, but now, thoughts of her flooded his brain. He could still smell her scent, as if she'd left something of herself with him when she'd walked past. Her eyes were burned into his memory, such an unusual shade in such an exotic face, and the single jewel bindi between them had only added to her mysterious allure. She was like a rare flower, seemingly unobtainable but all the more desirous because of the challenge. He recalled the regal way in which she'd walked, head held high, chin raised slightly, almost in a sign of aloof indifference, as if nothing and no one could touch her. It was a potent and challenging attraction to a man such as himself.

He shifted in his seat uncomfortably. *Fuck, I have to get out of here and do something physical!* The problem was the physical activity he wanted wasn't found at the gym.

He packed his briefcase and called Sanjay to pick him up. Perhaps he'd call Marla. He'd ask where she was currently located and see if she could make a stop through New Delhi. She'd at least take the edge off and provide the release he needed. In Australia, he had a number of willing women whom he often called upon, and they would also call on him if they felt the need. It was how he liked things — free from obligation and expectations.

Alex stepped out into the busy New Delhi street just as Sanjay pulled to a stop. Alex motioned for him to remain in the driver's seat and opened the back door himself. It always irritated him a little to have someone open doors for him. He expected it was because it questioned his masculinity and made him look like a lazy bastard. He settled himself in the backseat and asked Sanjay to take him directly to the hotel. He usually used his time in the car to read the news or his messages and it was immensely easier than navigating the Delhi traffic himself. A quick check of his mobile revealed that nothing important needed his immediate attention and he relaxed somewhat. He chuckled inwardly as he took note of the new additions that Sanjay had made to the hire car. A Ganesha figurine swung from the rearview mirror and some sort of incense bottle had been stuck to the dashboard. There was also an array of local magazines protruding from one of the seat pockets with various Indian celebrities splashed over the covers. Alex had forgotten his driver's penchant for gossip, even for gossip about people he'd never met. A quick assessment told him that Sanjay had also bought the bottles of water that he'd asked him to, and various packets of biscuits. Whenever he visited India, he gave those out to the beggars. Fresh drinking water was often hard to come by, particularly in summer. He also gave the biscuits to the women and children. While he wouldn't give money, as that was a recipe for disaster and often didn't end up in the hands of those who asked, at least he could give them some sustenance. He'd also asked Sanjay to run some errands for him that morning.

"Sanjay, did you purchase the thumb drive and the printer paper I need?"

"Yes, Boss. I put the bag in your backside!"

"I don't know how I could have missed it," Alex retorted dryly and chuckled.

Sooner than he'd expected, they were pulling up in front of the Totally Five Star. Alex breathed a sigh of relief. The heat and dust had started to get to him. The air conditioner in the offices where he'd been working that morning was not adequate for the space and had kept shutting off due to the numerous power outages that New Delhi suffered every day. He gave some quick instructions to Sanjay then stepped from the car and made his way quickly into the cool, expansive lobby. He loosened his tie and strode to the elevator banks. He would have forgone the tie entirely but for some meetings with the company management that morning. Tomorrow he'd ditch it since it was just too hot to stand on such ceremony. He keyed in his security code and closed his eyes in relief as the elevator started a rapid ascent. He could almost hear the cool water of the pool calling to him.

* * * *

Tanvi pushed back from her desk and massaged the tight muscles in her shoulders. The finance offices were located at the back of the ground floor. They had a view over one of the hotel's pools and she sometimes found herself daydreaming as she stared out at the beautiful, clear water. She was doing just that, staring out of the window, lost in thought, when someone stepped into her line of vision. She swiveled her chair to get a better look and sucked in her breath. It was the gentleman she'd seen at breakfast that morning. She knew it was him, even from the distance — his golden sun-streaked hair and strong physique immediately gave him away. He was striding purposefully toward the deep end, a towel and water bottle swinging from one hand. Tanvi glanced over her shoulder to ensure she was alone then scooted her chair closer to the window. The man had reached his destination and was circling his powerful shoulders and stretching his neck from side to side in a warm-up exercise. His chest was solid muscle and tan, and it undulated deliciously with his movements. Her gaze traveled lower to his hard abdomen and she licked her lips. Never had she seen such a man before. He was all power and masculinity. He'd donned what she assumed to be special swimming bathers, which clung to his buttocks like a second skin and molded to the impressive package between his legs. Her cheeks heated as her gaze lingered there, but, from her distance, she couldn't make out much. What she could see would surely make any woman hot and bothered. Even his legs looked strong, the muscles bulging and flexing as he moved. He bent at the waist and dove into the pool fluidly, his body barely making a splash when he hit the water. She found herself holding her breath until he broke the surface and began to swim, surging through the water with long, powerful strokes. She recalled earlier at breakfast his hard gaze as he'd stared at her, unapologetically undressing her with his eyes. This was a powerful man. This was an alpha male.

Tanvi sat back in her chair, aware of an unfamiliar feeling taking root low in her belly. She shuddered and her nipples peaked as arousal flooded her. Moisture gathered between her thighs and she wriggled in her seat in an attempt to stop the overwhelming onslaught of sensation. She was not a virgin by any means, but neither had she ever experienced such an overpowering allure to a man. She'd liberated herself of her virginity when she'd been studying in America, where sex was not a dirty word and people were not considered immoral for enjoying the act outside of marriage. But that had been more to do with an act of rebellion and self-discovery than any real feelings of lust. She supposed that she couldn't consider herself very sexually experienced either. Unlike Riya, who was outgoing and a bit of a risk taker, Tanvi had invariably stepped through life carefully, always mindful of her family's expectations. She sighed. Was her life always to be so devoid of passion and lust? If her family had their way, the answer was a depressing yes.

Another look out of the window confirmed that the man was still swimming laps. She guessed that he must have swum at least a dozen and he didn't appear to be slowing down. His strokes remained steady and strong, driving him through the water like a professional athlete. She sighed again, determined to start on another erotic novel at the first opportunity. Perhaps some personal time with a hunky book hero might assuage the needy throb that had settled in her belly, a feeling that left her both elated and depressed in equal measures. Elated, because she'd never experienced something quite so intense before, and depressed, because she was afraid that she might never have the feeling again.

She looked at her watch then started packing up her desk. She needed to get changed and meet Riya for their yoga class. Perhaps a little exercise would rid her of the pesky sensations invading her body.

Chapter Four

When Alexander had arrived back in his suite, he'd been pleasantly surprised to find that Deepak had ironed all his business shirts and polished his shoes, and when Alex had changed into his workout gear, Deepak had immediately whisked away the clothes he'd worn that day to wash and iron them. Alex had decided against dining in one of the hotel's renowned restaurants. He hated dining alone and had asked Deepak to make him an omelet instead, a request with which the little valet had enthusiastically complied.

Now he was sitting in the Totally Five Star lobby bar, enjoying a cold beer. He'd swum twenty laps and had worked out with weights and the bag in the gym and his muscles were feeling gratifyingly overused. It meant, hopefully, that he'd sleep well and keep his baser urges at bay, at least for a while. He'd left a message on Marla's phone, telling her where he was and how long he expected to be in New Delhi and he hoped that her modeling schedule would allow her a brief stopover.

He was texting his contracts manager when he felt *her* enter his periphery. He couldn't say *how* he knew it was she. Perhaps it was the subtle scent of her perfume, or the way the air shifted as she walked past his table. He looked up from his mobile and, sure enough, Tanvi Sharma was taking a seat a few tables away. She looked different. She'd twisted her hair into a thick, messy topknot and her beautiful eyes were lined with a softer color. She'd swapped the traditional *saree* for tight denim jeans that clung to her curves, her lush ass perfectly outlined as she bent to sit.

Fuck, she's a walking wet dream.

The saree she'd worn earlier had hidden her other assets, but he was treated to an eyeful of a perfect rack when she leaned forward, her sheer blouse barely concealing the jiggle of her plump breasts. He suppressed a groan as he gazed at her, his cock stiffening painfully against his jeans. Christ, the hard work he'd put in to douse his sexual urges had just been soundly obliterated.

Alex drummed his fingers on the tabletop, thinking about his next move. He had to approach her — he *needed* to. There was something about the woman that pulled him. Perhaps it was her exotic looks, or the graceful and confident way she moved? He didn't know, but what he did know was that he wouldn't rest until he'd made her acquaintance.

Tanvi saw him before she and Riya entered the bar. She couldn't mistake his sun-burnished hair and the relaxed, almost indolent way he was sitting in his chair, as if the world was ready to serve him. He was texting on his mobile phone, a beer at his elbow and the ankle of one long leg resting on his knee in a typical male stance.

She paused briefly before making her way past him to a nearby table. Thankfully, Riya hadn't appeared to notice him and was still chatting about their yoga class. Her relief was short-lived, however, as not long after they took their seats, she sensed his approach. Tanvi kept her eyes trained on the table, her heart beating a frantic tattoo in her chest. Why did the man have this effect on her? It was disturbing and alien and she had no idea what to do with the sensations. Riya paused in her prattle and kicked her shin. Tanvi frowned but kept her eyes down, not wanting to encourage the man.

"Ladies." His voice was deep and he had an accent that she couldn't place but that made him even more appealing.

"Hello," Riya greeted him, her tone flirtatious and inviting.

Tanvi scowled at her. *How can she get so much provocation into one word?*

"I hope you don't mind, but I took the liberty of ordering for you." He placed two champagne flutes on the table, each with a strawberry perched on the rim.

"Thank you. That's very kind," Riya breathed. "Won't you join us?"

"Only if your friend is agreeable. I don't want to intrude."

Tanvi felt another kick to her shin and glanced across the table at Riya, who was arching her eyebrows and giving her a pointed look. Tanvi raised her gaze to the man and realized how tall he actually was now that he was looming over them. She guessed his height to be over six feet and thought he'd dwarf most of the men she knew who tended toward a slighter, shorter build.

"Of course. Please do," she murmured.

He pulled out the chair next to hers and lowered himself fluidly into it. For such a tall, powerfully built man, he was certainly graceful with it. There was nothing remotely awkward or uncoordinated about him. He was supremely confident and self-assured.

He extended a hand to her. "I'm Alexander Banks. My friends call me Alex."

She took his hand. "Tanvi Sharma."

"I'm Riya." Riya thrust a hand in his direction. "I love your accent. Where are you from?"

"I'm Australian. I'm here on business."

"Ohhh. I love Australians," Riya gushed. "*Crocodile Dundee*."

Alexander chuckled. "Well, we all don't run around wearing Akubras and hunting crocodiles. Most of us are boringly normal guys."

He's anything but normal. Tanvi's mind wandered to what she'd witnessed that afternoon. No *normal* guys she knew had the physical stature and commanding presence that so easily emanated from Alexander Banks. And the ease with which he'd churned through the water had slightly astounded her. Only athletes and cricket players seemed to her to have that type of sporting prowess.

"How long are you here for?" Riya asked.

"I'm not sure yet. I'm staying here at the hotel. Perhaps a few weeks."

Riya fired another question at him. "Do you travel a lot?"

"Yes. Quite a bit."

"You must get lonely."

Tanvi cringed inwardly at Riya's blatant flirting, but it wasn't Riya he'd addressed his answer to.

"I do," he said quietly. "I particularly dislike dining alone."

Tanvi sucked in a breath and a shiver rippled down her spine as his ice-blue eyes bored into hers.

"Tanvi would be happy to have dinner with you, wouldn't you, Tanvi?"

Tanvi glared at Riya, who had gone too far. How dare she extend a dinner invitation on her behalf to a man she barely knew.

"As it happens, I wouldn't," Tanvi responded coolly. "You must forgive my friend. She gets a little carried away at times. I'm not in the habit of dining with strange men."

Alex took a sip of his beer and studied her, his inscrutable expression sending another shudder through her.

"I would appreciate the opportunity of getting to know you. What better way to start than over dinner?" His deep voice swept through her, resonating low in her belly, and it took all of her self-control to maintain her cool demeanor.

"I'm sorry, Mr. Banks, but the answer is no."

He leaned back in his chair and assessed her a moment longer, rolling his beer bottle between his thumb and forefinger.

"Very well," he said abruptly and stood. "I'll let you ladies get back to your evening." He nodded at them both and strode out of the bar, not glancing behind him but walking directly to the elevator bank.

"Are you kidding?" Riya all but screeched at her. "An off-the-scale, sexy-as-hell man just asked you to dinner and you turned him down with not even a whisper of an apology?"

"Keep your voice down!" Tanvi demanded. "And I *did* say *sorry*."

Riya glared at her, arms crossed in irritation. "Tanvi, I can't believe you didn't jump at the chance."

"I know nothing about the man. But more than that, you know it's impossible. What's the point of having dinner with him when I know that nothing can come of it?"

Riya heaved a sigh of frustration. "It's just dinner, Tanvi. I hardly think he'll be extending a marriage proposal, but *you* might get some extracurricular activity." She wriggled her eyebrows suggestively.

"And what would happen when someone sees us together? My life wouldn't be worth living."

Riya grasped her hand across the table. "Sweetie, some things are just worth risking. In your situation, I would be jumping — feet first! What better way to get rid of some of that pent-up sexual frustration than with a no-strings-attached affair?"

Tanvi frowned. She was never totally comfortable with Riya's openness about sex. Riya really was living in the wrong country and Tanvi supposed that was why she had begged her parents to look for a match for her in England or America. She was dying to get out of India and Tanvi felt for her. She too often felt weighed down by the oppressiveness of expectations.

"How do you know I'm sexually frustrated?" Tanvi finally murmured, curiosity getting the better of her.

Riya gave her a pointed look. "You're too serious and too tightly wound. To be honest, I don't know how you haven't snapped already! You need a release and, I think, a little excitement in your life. That Australian would set fire to your sheets. I guarantee it!"

Riya could have a point. "Can you email me the titles of those books you were recommending?"

Her friend grinned. "Of course, but you have the real deal ready and waiting."

"He was probably just being polite," Tanvi argued.

"Not from where I was sitting. Trust me. That man is hot for you."

"Excuse me, Ms. Sharma?"

Tanvi looked up at the waiter standing by their table. "Yes?"

"You have a message," he said, setting an envelope on the table before her.

Tanvi picked up the envelope and frowned. Who would leave her a message here?

"I bet it's from him." Riya bounced in her seat. "Open it."

She opened the flap and slid a card out of the envelope.

I'm 'sorry', Ms. Sharma, but the word 'no' is not in my vocabulary. Dinner tomorrow night. Meet me in the lobby at 7:30.
Alexander Banks

"Oh, my God," Riya gushed. "He's just so forthright and dominant. I told you he was an alpha male!"

Tanvi rolled her eyes. "I really wish you would stop reading so many of those novels. They're making you crazy."

"Are you going to go?"

"What do you think?"

"*I* think *you* should think about it! Live a little, girl. If you don't go, I might go in your place."

There was something about that idea that left a tight knot in Tanvi's belly. She didn't want Riya to have dinner with Alexander Banks. She loved her friend, but the thought of Riya with Alexander left a sour taste in her mouth and, she realized with a start, she was jealous.

"I might accept," she said finally.

Riya laughed. "He hardly invited you but told you."

"Well, we'll see what happens. Perhaps you're right and I need to live a little."

After all, I have all day tomorrow to work up the courage or decide just not to turn up, and the indomitable Mr. Banks can then go and find some other woman to have dinner with.

Tanvi looked at her watch. "It's getting late. Let's have one more champagne then call it a night."

Riya smirked at Tanvi and called over the waiter. "Let's toast to hunky Australians!"

Chapter Five

Alex was pissed! He'd felt in control until he'd seen *her* in the bar. She was all lush ass, round hips and plump breasts — and little! He had a thing about petite women. Perhaps it was a protection instinct that overcame him or it appealed to his dominant nature. He didn't know, nor did he want to analyze it. He just knew that he wanted Tanvi Sharma, more so than he'd wanted any woman.

He'd called down to the reception desk and left a message for her. It was unlike him to chase after a woman, but he wasn't going to give up so easily, which just made him even angrier. He was breaking all his rules with this one.

He stripped out of his clothes and wandered into the massive bathroom. After stepping into the two-person shower, he turned it on, relishing the blast of frigid water that doused him. He squirted soap into his hands and rubbed them together to form a lather. He thought about Tanvi's plump breasts and how they'd jiggled when she moved. The thought of her bountiful assets sent his cock springing to attention so it stood hard and erect against his abdomen. He groaned, needing to release some tension. He fisted his cock, pumping his palm over the thick organ roughly. He propped himself on one hand against the tiles and pulled his cock harder, the soap lubricating his glide. He imagined taking one of Tanvi's nipples into his mouth and sucking on the taut bud before kissing his way across to her other breast to give that nipple the same treatment. Could she come like that, he wondered, just from attention to her breasts? He moaned, squeezing the thick root of his cock then gliding his fist to the tip. He pulled harder, the squelching sounds of his palm and the soap loud, even over the cascade of water. He leaned back against the tiles and grabbed his balls with his other hand, fondling the sacs and groaning loudly. Lust coiled hot and taut at the base of his spine and his balls tightened as he neared his release. He gripped his ball sac harder and yanked his erection. He felt the cum bubbling through his cock and, with a low grunt, he climaxed. Thick streams of milky liquid pumped out of his tip as he fisted his cock to extend his orgasm. His erection was still rock-hard, his release only taking the edge off. He hated masturbating but sometimes it was necessary in order for him to keep his cool. He squeezed more soap into his hands and set to work on a second round. Fuck, if just the thought of her could get him so worked up, what would he do when he had her naked and tied to his bed?

* * * *

"It's time, Tanvi. You're twenty-five, most women are married by your age. Your uncle doesn't want you to wait any longer. The sooner you agree to marry Rakesh, the sooner the two families can combine. You know his father won't give me the contract for the financial services he needs until there's an official engagement."

Tanvi kept her head bent, tracing the floral pattern on the sofa with her index finger. She'd been using any excuse she could think of to put off her marriage to Rakesh. She couldn't stand the man. He was a misogynist and was verbally cruel, but in front of her parents, his behavior had always been above reproach, and she'd been unable to convince them otherwise. Why couldn't they have arranged a marriage for her with a nicer man? Her life as she knew it would soon be over, so she decided then and there that she would meet Alexander Banks for dinner. She had nothing to lose, so why not at least have some fun before there was no fun to be had? If she was careful, no one would be any the wiser. She knew her father feared what her uncle could do with his connections, and getting on the wrong side of him could be dangerous. However, just once she'd wished her father would stand up to him. She knew that her uncle expected to get something out of her union with Rakesh but Tanvi didn't know what exactly.

She also had another concern—what would Rakesh do when he found out she wasn't a virgin? Men in India preferred their wives to be intact and Rakesh was definitely the type of man to expect that. She'd read about women having their hymens repaired but that seemed a bit extreme. No, Rakesh would just have to live with it—the thought pleased her.

She sighed and got to her feet. She didn't respond to her father. She understood that no verbal acknowledgment was required of her. Her father had spoken and, in his mind, his word was law.

She went to her room and closed the door before opening her closet and inspecting the contents. She'd purchased a silk dress from a local designer and she'd been waiting for an occasion to wear it. It was a little lower cut than she generally wore but it was sexy and made her feel sophisticated and feminine.

Yes, this is perfect. Alexander will love this!

Chapter Six

Alexander had worked steadily through the day. It was three o'clock and he was pleased that he'd had time to get a workout in. He hadn't seen Tanvi all day. He'd left the hotel early and supposed that he'd missed her arrival so was none the wiser as to whether she'd accepted his dinner invitation. Alex had hoped that seeing her might give him an idea as to her frame of mind but he'd just have to assume that she would be in the lobby at the appointed time. He'd booked the hotel rooftop restaurant, which was rated the highest in India, and the seating was comfortable and private.

He dressed in light tan-colored chinos and a white open-necked shirt, which he rolled to the elbows. He splashed aftershave on his face and stepped into a pair of casual Timberlands.

Alex strolled into the hotel lobby bar then ordered a beer. He chose a table that gave him a direct view of the entrance. He drummed his fingers on the table, impatience tightening his chest. He hated the impotent feelings this woman wrought within him. He hadn't even thought about what he'd do if she didn't turn up. He supposed there was nothing much he could do. She wasn't his submissive. He had no power over her actions, another reason for his irritation. He'd only met her once, so his strong feelings for her surprised him. She was exotically beautiful and had a body made for fucking, but there was something else about her. It was the way she held herself and moved, like nothing and no one could touch her. It was the challenge in the chase. He wanted her in his bed — needed it. He imagined gripping those curves and pulling that compact little body tight to his as he fucked her hard. He groaned inwardly and shifted in his seat, his cock stiffening in response to his thoughts. He glanced at his watch — seven-forty — she was late or not coming at all. He looked up as movement at the entrance caught his attention and there she was, her hair flowing down her back in a thick ebony veil. He was glad she'd worn it down. He'd been fantasizing about that gorgeous hair and what he could do with it. Her dress clung to her curves, the green color deepening the shade of her eyes. She hadn't lined them as heavily tonight, and the effect was less exotic but no less appealing.

He stood to greet her. "I'm glad you decided to come."

She nodded and looked around the bar. "Are we eating here?"

"No. I've made reservations at the rooftop restaurant."

She looked relieved. Perhaps the lobby was too public for her. The thought intrigued him. In his experience the Indian people didn't worry about privacy. In fact, it was largely a foreign concept, so why then would Tanvi look worried about the lack of it?

He placed his palm on the small of her back. "Why don't we go up now?"

She smiled, the effect lighting up her eyes and face. He determined there and then that he'd make her smile as often as possible. Whenever he'd seen her, she'd looked serious and a little sad. He ushered her into the elevator and pushed the button for the rooftop. He'd requested a table inside, deciding that the air-conditioned comfort would be more conducive to an enjoyable dinner.

Tanvi had never been to the rooftop restaurant. She'd heard about it, of course, but it was expensive and she hadn't had the justification to go. She was excited to try the food. It was rated number one in India and the chef was celebrated for his innovative Indian dishes. She'd also been happy that they were leaving the lobby. She didn't expect her parents or her uncle to turn up, but she couldn't rule out the possibility either. At least she wouldn't expect them to be dining at the restaurant. It wasn't something they would do without pre-planning and some momentous occasion to celebrate.

The elevator reached the rooftop and they stepped out. She was conscious of Alexander's large palm on her back. It was warm and strangely comforting. His aftershave, spicy and woodsy, wafted over her and tightened her nipples to taut peaks. She hoped the pattern in her dress hid her arousal. She felt slightly obscene but nonchalant with it. It was the first time in a long time she had experienced such free and easy emotions. At liberty to do what she wanted, she'd forget her parents, her uncle and Rakesh and what was expected of her and enjoy herself. Alexander Banks was an attractive man, masculinity oozing from him, and she noticed how other women stared at him with interest. But it wasn't only his attractiveness — he also had a commanding presence, that sexy alpha male quality.

Tanvi glanced around the restaurant. The décor was traditional Indian with a modern edge. The walls were painted beige, and paper in thick stripes of intricate gold was interspersed throughout. The upholstery was red and green and the same gold pattern adorning the walls was replicated in throw cushions in the dining alcoves. Palm trees in brass pots scattered around the restaurant provided an exotic addition and offered diners seclusion. Large ceiling fans oscillated quietly and sitar music played unobtrusively in the background. Waiters scurried around with platters of food and trays of drinks, the women draped in traditional sarees, the men in black pants and shirts.

They walked past a table of foreign businessmen and Tanvi could immediately sense their interest. They stopped talking and stared at her, their eyes undressing her hungrily. She felt Alexander's hold on her shift. He pulled her body tighter to his side and shot an angry glare at the table. She wasn't used to public displays of affection and she hardly knew Alexander. She should have felt embarrassed, but she wasn't. She felt secure in Alexander's hold, like she belonged there.

They reached their table and he pulled out her chair for her. Rakesh would never do the same thing. He would seat himself in the most comfortable position and forget that she was even at the table with him. He enjoyed having her on his arm, enjoyed her connections and looks, but didn't ever seem to *want* to be with her.

Tanvi smiled at Alexander across the table. "Thank you for the dinner invitation."

"It's me who should be thanking you. I'm very glad that you decided to accept. I hadn't worked out what my next move would be if you hadn't shown up tonight."

A waiter arrived and handed them each a menu.

"A bottle of your Veuve Clicquot, please." Alexander spoke to the waiter before turning his attention to Tanvi. "I hope that's all right with you?"

"Of course." Tanvi was flattered. Decent wine in India was expensive and the price of French champagne didn't bear thinking about. She perused her menu and noticed that there were no prices. How could she be expected to make an appropriate choice with no price to guide her? She bit her bottom lip in indecision and glanced across the table. Alexander had placed his menu to one side and was studying her, his lips tilted in a subtle smirk.

"The ladies menus have no prices," he explained. "We want you to make a choice based on what you like, without thinking about the cost."

"Ohh." Tanvi realized suddenly that she'd never before dined in such an exclusive restaurant. It was exciting and daunting in equal measure.

"Is there anything you don't like or can't eat?" Alexander asked.

"I'm allergic to peanuts. It's quite an uncommon allergy here, so I have to be careful."

Alexander nodded. "Shall I order for us? This restaurant is renowned for two dishes in particular, the Kaali Dal and the Raan Nawabi."

Tanvi put her menu aside and smiled. "Ahh, creamy black lentils and royal leg of lamb. I've heard of these dishes. I believe they are normally used as a festive meal because of the long marinating and cooking time."

"I haven't tried them myself. The previous times I've eaten here, I've eaten alone and I couldn't quite justify ordering the leg of lamb for myself. But as they are the restaurant's specialty and I'm not alone, and I believe in celebrating..."

"Now it all becomes clear, Mr. Banks." Tanvi smiled. "You only wanted my company so you could order the specialty dishes."

"Of course not," he said easily. "But I do believe you agreeing to have dinner with me calls for a celebratory feast."

The waiter returned with their champagne. They sat quietly while he poured each of them a glass. Another waiter appeared at their table with papadums and chutney and explained to them that there was no cutlery and that the food was to be eaten with their hands, using the bread accompaniment as a scoop.

Tanvi raised an eyebrow. "Not the most genteel meal, Mr. Banks. Are you trying to get me dirty?"

Chapter Seven

Alexander almost choked on his champagne. The way Tanvi called him Mr. Banks and the reference to getting her dirty? She had no idea how close he was to diving over the table and ravishing her. She'd hit all his buttons with one sentence. She really was an intriguing little minx. He would never have guessed that her cool demeanor could be so easily fired. It was an interesting turn of events. He leaned back in his chair, rolling the stem of his champagne glass between thumb and forefinger, assessing the woman opposite him. She wore a little smirk on her lips and was studying him from under lowered lashes. *Yes, she knows exactly what she's doing.*

The waiter appeared with their meal, breaking the fervent tension that had arisen between them. The dishes looked and smelled delicious. The leg of lamb wasn't big and had obviously been cooked over a number of hours. The waiter placed the platter between them and set to work deftly shredding the meat off the bone using two spoons. The dal was creamy and delicious and was placed next to a basket of crispy naan. The waiter explained the dishes, refilled their glasses and left them to eat.

"Well, if looks and this aroma are anything to go by, I believe we have a feast fit for a king. Shall we toast?" Alexander raised his glass.

"Of course," Tanvi agreed, raising her own. "To the Totally Five Star Hotel."

Alexander arched an eyebrow, but clinked his glass with Tanvi's. "I would have thought that a toast to us would be more appropriate," he murmured after taking a sip. "Isn't that the norm?"

"Precisely! It's too clichéd. Why not toast to the hotel that put us in each other's path?"

"You have a point," Alex concurred. "I, for one, despise clichés." He picked up Tanvi's plate and served her some of each of the two dishes before serving himself. When he looked up, she was smiling at him.

"You know, you are a true gentleman," she murmured, taking a piece of naan and breaking it into smaller pieces.

Alex raised his eyebrows in surprise. *If only you knew my true nature, baby. Perhaps you wouldn't think me such a gentleman.* He cleared his throat. "Women should always be treated like ladies." Fuck, could he get any cornier? He'd better hope that his initial assumptions were correct and that he was gaining ground with her and not coming across like a complete ass. He scooped up a mouthful of the delicious lamb. It was spicy and aromatic and melted in his mouth. It was easy to tell why the Totally Five Star was rated the number one Indian restaurant. He looked across at Tanvi, who was chewing delicately, her plump lips shiny from the rich meat. A drop of sauce lodged at the corner of her mouth. The whole erotic effect was wreaking havoc with his self-control. He very slowly leaned across the table and swiped at the drop of sauce with his thumb. He sucked it into his mouth. "Mmm, it tastes even better from your lips."

Her mouth formed a perfect 'O' and her eyes widened in surprise. He smirked at her, pleased that he'd put her off balance.

She cleared her throat and took a sip of champagne. "You said last night that you're here on business?"

"Yes, I'm looking at investing in a local company."

"Investing?"

"I own some companies in Australia. I sometimes invest in other companies, depending on what their capabilities can offer me. I have to get some advantages out of the deal after all." He shrugged. "It makes for dull dinner conversation."

"I don't find it dull. I find it interesting." She smiled.

When Tanvi smiled, her entire face lit up and stripped away the seriousness that too often seemed to color her features. He suspected there was a fiery temptress under that cool demeanor and he wanted to be the man to unleash it.

The waiter appeared and cleared their plates. "Would you like dessert, sir?"

Alex raised his eyebrow in inquiry at Tanvi, who shook her head and looked at her watch. "The food was delicious but I've eaten far too much and I have to work tomorrow."

Alex addressed the waiter. "Thank you. That will be all."

He stood and stepped around the table to pull Tanvi's chair out for her. "Shall we go? I don't want you to miss your beauty sleep."

She rose and shot him a mock glare. "Alexander, are you suggesting that I need it?"

"Of course not." He picked up her hand and kissed her palm. He hadn't missed her use of his first name and he hoped it meant that she was warming toward him. "You are incredibly beautiful. In fact, you're one of the most beautiful women I have ever met."

She blushed and started fussing with her handbag. "Thank you," she finally said, the words so softly spoken that he barely heard them. "What about the bill?" she asked suddenly, a flush coloring her features.

He'd made prior arrangements to have it added to his room service charge, along with a hefty tip. "It's taken care of." He wrapped an arm around her waist and led her to the exit and the elevators. "How did you get here?"

"The usual way, by tuk tuk."

Alex shot her a surprised look. "Your family doesn't have a car and a driver? Someone once told me that everyone has a driver in India" — he chuckled — "and that even the drivers have drivers."

Tanvi threw her head back and laughed, a light tinkling sound that immediately disarmed him. She was carefree and joyous and it transformed her. He looked around the rooftop and quickly drew her aside and into a darkened alcove. He ignored her gasp of surprise and urged her farther into the dim recess.

Tanvi gasped in shock as Alexander pressed her against the brick, her back flush with the warm cement. Before she could say or do anything, he grasped both her hands in one of his and pushed them above her head. Her heart beat a rapid tattoo against her ribs. She tipped her head back and eyed him warily. He was looking at her intently, his ice-blue eyes boring into hers from above.

He dropped his head until she felt his lips against her ear. "Shhh," he whispered.

His cologne, all woodsy and masculine, wafted around her and she relaxed slightly and closed her eyes. He traced his lips across her cheek to her mouth, his breath whisper soft against her skin. Her nipples pebbled and hot desire sluiced through her veins. She waited for Alexander to take her mouth, but he hovered there, a hair's breadth from her lips.

Please!

Never had she felt such desire just from a man's proximity. His hard body was contrary to her softer one—a wall of solid muscle. She should have felt afraid but her initial fear had turned to pure want. Then, finally, his lips were on hers, soft but firm and demanding, so demanding as he took her mouth in a powerful kiss. All thought deserted her and she succumbed to his will, urging her body tighter to his. She heard a moan and realized with a start that it came from her. He swallowed the sound as he slanted his lips roughly across hers, invading her mouth with his tongue. He kept her hands imprisoned, preventing her movement. Her mind, made fuzzy through lust and champagne, grasped one thought—it was so hot! If he could make her feel like this, he could hold her captive whenever he wanted. His free hand was at her breast, caressing the side lightly before he smoothed it lower, over her waist until he grasped her hip and pulled her pelvis tightly to his. She could feel his erection between them, hot and thick and *pulsing*. She moaned again, uncaring of their location, and raised her thigh, desperate to feel his throbbing at her core. Her dress restricted her movement and she groaned her frustration. He slowed his assault on her mouth and kissed a trail down her throat before sweeping her dress a little higher up her thighs. Then he was lifting her, his hand on her backside and his thick erection at her sex, grinding into her exactly where she needed it. She gasped her pleasure before he took her lips once more, his mouth demanding and powerful. Tanvi had never felt such desire, such overwhelming sensations. She didn't want it to stop. Every thought but those of lust and longing had been swept from her brain. All too soon, he pulled away from her, sliding her body slowly down his until her feet touched the ground once more. He dropped his forehead to hers and swore softly through his panting breaths. She couldn't speak, still too winded and woozy.

Alexander released her hands and rubbed his thumb over her lips. "Your mouth is swollen from my kiss," he muttered, his voice low and rough. He fixed her dress then stooped and picked up her handbag from the ground where she'd dropped it. "I'd better get you home."

His last sentence broke through the fog in her brain. "You can't take me home," she said. "I'll make my own way."

"I'm not happy about that. I never allow a woman to make her own way home."

Tanvi wondered just how many women he was talking about, but she quickly banished the thought. Now was not the time to speculate about Alexander's sexual conquests.

"I'm fine," she said determinedly, punching the button for the elevator. "I live here and I'm constantly traveling around the city at all hours of the night."

The elevator arrived and they stepped in. "At least let me have Sanjay drive you. He's waiting out the front in case I needed him tonight. It will put my mind at ease."

Tanvi thought quickly. If her parents saw, she could explain Sanjay away as a friend's brother. "Fine," she agreed.

They'd reached the lobby and Tanvi quickened her step, suddenly feeling the need to put distance between herself and Alexander, but before she could go very far, he grasped her hand and tugged her back. *Please don't kiss me.* She looked at him warily.

"Have dinner with me tomorrow night." He ran a hand through his hair, mussing it sexily. "Please," he murmured. "I want to see you again."

"Give me your business card," she said quickly. "I'll call you."

He narrowed his eyes but reached into a pocket and extracted a white card embossed with gold lettering. "I'd prefer to call you," he said, his voice brimming with irritation. "How can I contact you?"

"I assume from your lack of inquiry regarding my profession that you're aware that I'm working here."

He gave a brisk nod.

She smiled and turned once more toward the exit. "I'll be in touch," she called over her shoulder before stepping out into the sultry night air.

Chapter Eight

All morning Tanvi had been reliving her dinner with Alexander. More than once George had had to nudge her out of her daydreaming to the point where it was becoming embarrassing.

She couldn't quite believe the way that Alexander had taken total control of her emotions *and* her body. It was as if he'd cast some sort of spell over her. She'd never been an impulsive or passionate woman and, if anything, she had always been considered cold, and had even once, cruelly and unjustifiably, been dubbed a cock-teasing prude. She'd reached a point in life where she believed the unflattering adjectives associated with her character. After all, she'd never felt the remotest glimmer of sexual lust or want, not toward any man she'd met at any rate. She hadn't considered that perhaps she just hadn't encountered the *right* man to evoke those emotions in her. Now, she was positive that she had and she was determined to experiment further. She wouldn't enter into a loveless, passionless marriage without first having experienced toe-curling, true abandonment. She wanted first-hand knowledge, something to keep her going through the difficult years she expected were ahead of her.

It was useless. She was unable to concentrate and concentration was imperative when she was working with numbers. "I'm sorry, George, but I don't think I'm fit to do any more work today."

George gave her a fatherly pat on the back. "You haven't been yourself today. You work too hard. It's Friday, take an early weekend."

She packed up her things and thought about what she was going to text to Alexander. She hadn't called him and she was mildly surprised that he hadn't resolved to contact her first—he didn't strike her as the most patient man. She'd already decided what she wanted to suggest they do for the evening. She'd made inquiries with reception under the guise of a billing discrepancy and confirmed that Alexander was staying in one of their suites, which meant that he had a kitchenette. She wanted to cook for him. She loved to cook and could often be found in their home kitchen with their housekeeper, Monica, helping her with the family meals and learning all of her delicious recipes. It also meant that they would be safe from prying eyes. She preferred not to dwell on the fact that they would also be alone and uninhibited in Alexander's hotel room. She'd never before suggested anything so forward and she hoped that he wouldn't regard her as being too presumptuous.

Before she could lose her nerve, she texted him with her suggestion and, not waiting for a reply, she left the hotel for the markets where she would purchase her ingredients.

Alexander couldn't help but check his phone. He couldn't risk missing an important business-related email but it also meant that he was continually confronted with the fact that Tanvi hadn't contacted him. He refused to call her. The ball was squarely in her court now. He'd already spent more time than he ever had with any other woman in pursuing and wooing Tanvi. His masculinity would be called into question if he invested in too much more romantic persuasion. He was a dominant man, but he certainly hadn't been acting like one. More like a lust-driven schoolboy, he thought disgustedly. His mind drifted to the previous evening and how Tanvi had surprised and delighted him with her sensuality and passion. He'd been right — there was definitely a fiery temptress under that cool demeanor. In fact, she'd seemed surprised herself by her reactions to him, which was an intriguing development.

His phone dinged, alerting him to a text message. He didn't check it immediately. Determined to exert some self-control, he forced himself to sit through a further half hour of technical discussions. When he determined the time was right, he pulled up his text messages and was more relieved than he cared to admit when he saw the message was from her. He read it with increasing astonishment, then read it again to assure himself he wasn't imagining the text. Well, she'd surprised him again and he found himself enjoying the emotion. He'd never been a big one for surprises, but Tanvi Sharma was doing a remarkable job of changing that aspect of his nature. She wanted to cook for him, in his suite no less, and would be at his door at seven-thirty with the supplies. The opportunities that this development presented ran fast and furiously through his brain. He was amazed that she'd been so bold as to propose it but he suspected there was another reason for her actions and he'd do well to remember that. At any rate, he'd have her to himself in the privacy of his suite and the knowledge sent expectant tension humming through his system.

He called the meeting to a close, citing the fact that he wanted his managers' input when they arrived on Monday. He packed his laptop and paperwork into his briefcase and called for Sanjay. He replied to Tanvi's message while he was in the car, a quick text saying he was looking forward to dinner and he'd see her at seven-thirty.

Twenty minutes later, Alex entered his suite at the Totally Five Star. He asked Deepak to organize flowers, candles and a bottle of the hotel's best champagne, then he gave him the rest of the afternoon and evening off. Before he left, Alex issued him with strict instructions not to return to the suite on Saturday unless he was called for. Perhaps he was getting a little ahead of himself but he was covering all bases. He wasn't a man who had gotten to be where he was without meticulous planning and risk management.

He strode into his bedroom and was pleased to note that everything was in order, as was the rest of the suite. He changed into his workout gear, having decided to do a few laps then perhaps some weights. He needed to loosen up after sitting for hours in meetings, and working off some sexual tension wouldn't hurt either.

Alex swam twenty laps and spent thirty minutes in the gym. When he arrived back at his suite, he felt invigorated and flush with endorphins. He'd cut his usual routine a little short, but it had been enough to leave him feeling energized after an inactive day of sitting around.

The flowers had been delivered and unlit candles were placed strategically around the suite. A bottle of French champagne sat chilling in a silver ice bucket at the end of the dining room table. Deepak had done well, perhaps having surmised that Alex was expecting female company.

He had an hour until Tanvi was due to arrive. He strode into the bathroom and turned on the shower.

Chapter Nine

Alexander lit the candles, dimmed the sitting area lights and scanned through his iPod for something romantic. He had thousands of bands and songs for all different occasions. He selected a Michael Bublé album, not one of his favorites, but he expected Tanvi to appreciate it. He surveyed the suite and hoped it didn't project as trying too hard. He wanted Tanvi to feel comfortable and appreciated, and he'd already won points for the gentlemanly approach, so he decided to stick with it.

The doorbell rang at precisely seven-thirty. Tanvi Sharma was punctual—that pleased him.

He opened the door and paused on the threshold, sucking in a breath. Tanvi stood there, swathed in a white saree edged in gold. The pure white of the fabric contrasted beautifully with her caramel skin. Her hair hung down her back in a thick braid and she'd placed a red spot between her eyes—a bindi.

"You look beautiful," he murmured.

"Thank you." She indicated the bags at her feet. "The supplies."

Alex stepped out and waved her forward. "Please. I'll get the bags."

Tanvi walked into Alexander's suite. She was gratified at how hard he'd worked to make the ambience romantic. She'd never been into one of the suites and she took a moment to look around. The interior decoration was modern but comfortable. The colorful Indian artwork on the wall was enhanced by the neutral shades of the furnishings and the cotton rugs on the floor provided an authentic feel. She walked through the dining area where more candles shimmered and a bottle of champagne was chilling.

Alexander appeared behind her. "The kitchenette is through here." He strode past her and into a doorway at the end of the room.

Tanvi followed him into a small but functional kitchen. There was a stovetop with three gas burners, an oven and a microwave. She opened a few cupboards and found them stocked with all sorts of appliances. She'd have no problems cooking for Alexander in this kitchen. In the bottom cupboards she found a fine bone china dinner set and matching platters, all of the ceramics edged in twenty-four karat gold and decorated with palm trees and elephants. It was an expensive set and would ensure that the meal she was cooking was served in style.

She set about unpacking her bags and transferring the cold items to the refrigerator. She'd woken early that morning and made the coconut spice mixture for the curry, having decided the previous evening that she wanted to cook for Alexander.

Tanvi retrieved potatoes, eggplant and zucchini and started to slice the vegetables into thin rounds.

She whipped up a batter with *besan* and water, a pinch of chili powder and seasoning and put a deep pan on the stovetop to heat. Next, she took the marinating chicken from the fridge and started to heat another pan. She'd decided to cook a Southern Indian curry and as soon as the chicken started to sizzle, the scent of coconut and spices wafted up, telling her that her masala was just the right mixture of aromatics.

Alex leaned against a bench top and watched Tanvi as she moved gracefully around the kitchen, the saree tied low on her hips, enhancing the roundness of her ass. She seemed at home and comfortable in the domesticity and he found himself enjoying the scene. Other than dinner at his parents' home, he couldn't recall the last time someone had cooked for him.

"What are you making?" he asked, intrigued.

She looked up. "Vegetable pakora. Our housekeeper, Monica, makes them for us. There would always be a fresh batch of these waiting for me when I got home from school." She smiled. "Whenever I eat them, it reminds me of those days."

She dipped the vegetable rounds into the batter then slipped them into the shimmering pot of oil. Almost immediately a mouthwatering aroma filled the air.

Alex started to collect cutlery and plates. "I'll set the table."

"I'll be in with the food in a few moments."

Alex strode into the dining area, set the table and popped the cork on the champagne then poured the bubbly liquid into two crystal glasses. A moment later,

Tanvi appeared with a steaming platter of pakora, which she placed on the table.

Alex pulled a chair out for her then took a seat opposite. Tanvi picked up the platter and offered it to him. He chose a pakora and bit into it. It was delicious, lightly spiced and crunchy. "I can see why these are such a fond childhood memory, they're extremely tasty."

"They're not particularly healthy. They're deep fried after all." She shrugged. "But you need to try them at least once."

Alex selected a second eggplant version. "The saree you're wearing tonight. It's unusual, not as colorful as the others."

"It's typical of South India. That's where my mother comes from."

"It suits you. It's very elegant."

She smiled. "I thought it was appropriate seeing as I'm making a Goan chicken curry. In fact, it should be ready now. I'll go and plate it up."

Alex poured each of them another glass of champagne and took another pakora. They truly were delicious and the aroma of coconut and spices that was emanating from the kitchen told him that the curry would be just as tasty.

Tanvi arrived back at the table with a platter of chicken and steamed rice. She placed it on the table between them with a flourish. "Ta-da!"

He chuckled. She looked so different when she was carefree and she smiled, as if some sort of weight had been lifted from her shoulders.

She'd sprinkled the food with coriander and the scent of the fresh herbs with the spicy coconut made his mouth water. She served him some chicken and rice before helping herself.

Alex found himself enjoying the domestic and relaxed ease of the evening, as if they'd been dining together for years. It was exhilarating and disturbing in equal measures. He was unaccustomed to such sentimental emotions. Typically, he didn't wine and dine the women he fucked and they definitely didn't cook for him, but Tanvi was different. He'd understood that from the moment he'd set eyes on her. He'd known instinctively that the only way to get anywhere with her would be to take the gentlemanly approach and he was mildly surprised that he'd had the patience to follow it through. But she was an itch that he had to scratch. She'd worked her way under his skin and he couldn't rest until he had remedied the situation.

He assessed her across the table. She really was beautiful. She'd outlined her eyes again with the black kohl and he realized that she did it when she was dressed in the traditional fashion. It enhanced her exotic appearance and the hazel green of her eyes.

"You're very quiet. Do you like the curry?"

Alex startled and realized with embarrassment that he'd been staring at her while he ate. "I'm sorry, I was lost in thought. The chicken is delicious. You're a fabulous cook."

She blushed. "Thank you. I'm glad you're enjoying it."

"I'm intrigued. I recall you telling me that you're allergic to peanuts. Coconut doesn't bother you?"

"No. Despite its name, it's actually classified as a fruit." She shrugged. "I think some sources classify it as a tree nut but apparently most tree nut allergy sufferers can eat coconut. I'm glad because it's fabulous in a curry."

Alex ate two more mouthfuls then placed his knife and fork together on his plate. "I'm full and extremely satisfied. I really appreciate it. I can't remember when someone last cooked for me."

She looked up from collecting the dishes. "Really?"

He shrugged. "The women...I associate with are not really cooks."

"Oh."

Her expression was pensive and he decided to change the subject.

"I'll help you clear." He stood and started to collect the plates, his mind working furiously. He needed to get an idea of her expectations for the evening. Had she just planned to enjoy a lovely meal together and she'd be leaving in an hour? Or was she expecting more? He decided that Tanvi would appreciate a direct approach. She didn't seem like a woman who played games or enjoyed beating around the bush.

He followed her into the kitchen and stood behind her. He waited until she'd placed the dishes in the sink, then he caged her, his arms either side of her body. She stiffened then relaxed but stayed completely still.

He bent his head to speak softly in her ear. "Are you going to spend the night with me?"

Chapter Ten

Tanvi's mind raced with indecision. She appreciated Alex's candor, but it left the ball squarely in her court. She willed herself to relax. His arms were at either side of her, locking her against the bench top, his hard body pressed to her back. At such close proximity, she could feel his muscles. His powerful physique was emphasized, as were the differences in their height and build. His obvious strength was intoxicating. His body so near to hers was making it hard for her to think.

She decided she'd go with a part answer and let him make the next move. "I packed my toothbrush," she murmured.

His breath hitched. It was hot in her ear, the sensation peaking her nipples to painfully hard points.

"Good," he finally acknowledged, his deep voice washing over her, prompting her to relax further.

He banded one arm around her waist and tugged her against him. She could feel his thick erection throbbing against her lower back. He bent his knees and lifted her slightly to nestle his cock amid the cheeks of her ass.

"Feel this?" he asked thickly as he rubbed himself against her. "This is how much I want you."

Desire flared through her veins to settle and pool between her thighs. No other man had ever made her yearn for his touch—made her feel so needy.

His mouth was still at her ear, his breathing deep and even and at odds with her own rapid inhalations. "I want you to go into the bedroom off the living area and wait for me," he instructed and stepped away from her.

Tanvi took a moment to steady herself then did as he'd asked, escaping quickly into the bedroom. She needed a few minutes to gain her composure and was glad of the slight reprieve he'd given her.

Alex waited until Tanvi had followed his instructions, then he strode into the living area. He selected Enigma's *Sadeness* on the iPod docking station, turning the volume up until the eerie chants and music swelled and filled the suite. It had been around for a while, but he loved to fuck to it. He sat on the sofa and waited a couple of minutes. He needed to prolong the anticipation. He wanted Tanvi a little on edge and wondering what he was going to do to her. Also, he was in danger of racing into the bedroom and ripping that saree off her lush little body if he didn't take a few minutes to get his raging hormones under control. He wanted to take things slowly with her and savor every moment. This was not going to be a quick shag, not by any stretch. He intended to take his own sweet time with the luscious creature waiting for him in his room. He imagined unwrapping her until every inch of what he knew would be a gorgeous body was revealed to him. His cock pressed painfully against his jeans and he stood, unable to wait any longer.

Tanvi was standing at the foot of the bed, her bottom lip locked between her teeth. She was nervous and he enjoyed keeping her off balance. She'd done nothing but wait for him — that was good. She'd followed his instructions exactly.

He allowed his gaze to travel over her saree-swathed body and what he imagined to be meters of silk. Unwrapping her would be like opening the sweetest gift. She fidgeted, obviously uncomfortable under his steady observation.

"Don't move," he demanded.

She stilled immediately. Oh, she was perfect, perfectly submissive and obedient. His erection throbbed painfully, but he ignored the sensation, needing to focus all his attention on Tanvi.

He stepped toward her and studied the intricately wrapped saree. "Is there a trick to this?"

She raised her eyes to his. "May I?"

He nodded once, and she reached into the skirt and undid a large safety pin hidden between the folds. She tossed the pin aside and gave him a shy smile.

Alex raised his eyebrows in question and she nodded. He untucked a piece of fabric at her waist and pulled. Layers of material unfolded in white waves, her body spinning as he tugged until she stood in a cloud of silk, now clad only in a modest white cloth petticoat and her saree blouse. It was a sensual and beautiful act, unwrapping something so perfect, and he wished that he'd filmed it so he could replay it later.

A drawstring kept the petticoat in place. He untied the bow and tugged the skirt down. She turned and he unclasped the hooks and eyes of the blouse, opened it and pushed it off her shoulders. She wasn't wearing a bra and he closed his hands over the smooth mounds of her breasts, kneading until she moaned. He opened his hands and palmed her nipples to stiff peaks, dropping his head closer to hers and inhaling her sweet scent. Fuck, she was gorgeous.

She melted against him, her head resting on his shoulder as he manipulated her breasts, extending and elongating her nipples until he had to see his handiwork. He pushed her gently away from him and spun her around. Her heavy breasts bounced when she moved, her nipples standing high and erect. His breath hitched. He had to taste her. He bent his head to one breast and sucked the nipple deeply into his mouth. She groaned and pushed against him. He wrapped one arm around her waist, cupping her backside with the other, and picked her up so her breast was level with his mouth. He sucked harder, biting on her nipple until she shuddered in his arms.

Chapter Eleven

There was a fire in Tanvi's belly, burning low and hot and turning her insides into a quaking, trembling caldron of sensation. She threw her arms around Alexander's shoulders and pushed her breast harder into his mouth. He nibbled and sucked on her nipple, biting into her soft flesh. A flash of pleasurable pain streaked through her to land between her thighs and she jerked against him. Vaguely, she registered the eerie, chanting music as it swelled around them, adding to the haze taking over her brain.

Alexander walked them to the foot of the bed. He released her nipple and tossed her gently onto the mattress. He loomed over her and she could see the hunger and longing in his ice-blue eyes. It made her feel strangely powerful to have some sort of control over this strong, virile male. Moisture pooled between her thighs and she was afraid that her desire would show through her panties. She locked her legs together in sudden embarrassment.

He shook his head. "Never hide yourself from me, Tanvi. I want to see every inch of you." He grasped her ankles, spread her legs wide and crawled between them. She held her breath, unsure what he was going to do, then gasped in shock when he lowered his head, ran his nose over her panties and inhaled.

"Mmm, you smell so good."

Did he just do that? She was shocked but aroused at his blatant sexuality.

He slipped his thumbs under the elastic of her panties. "Lift that pretty little backside," he ordered then swept her panties down her legs and tossed them aside. He stared at her a moment and she was glad that she'd taken care to groom herself in readiness. Then, to her horror, he dropped his head and swiped his tongue through her center.

She squirmed away from him, but he gripped her hips and slapped her thigh lightly. "Stay still!"

"No one has ever..." She floundered, panicked. To her, that had always been the most intimate act. *Do I want to get that intimate with him?*

He looked up from between her legs, his eyes wide in surprise. "You're not a virgin, are you?"

"No, but no one has ever...done that."

He smirked at her. "I'm glad I'll be the first to have my mouth here. Relax and enjoy it. I need to loosen you up, prepare you."

Prepare me for what? But all thought fled her brain when he closed his mouth over her and sucked. She gasped and writhed beneath him, but he held her hips still. Nothing had ever felt so good. She let intimacy inhibitions fly and gave herself over to the sensations. He swiped his tongue along her cleft then plunged it into her channel, probing deeply. She moaned and opened her legs wider, thrusting her hips to match his rhythm. He licked at her, sweeping his tongue around and around her clit but not touching where she desperately needed it.

"Please, Alexander."

She tried to swivel her hips, but he held her fast. She grasped his hair and tried to force his head where she wanted it. He chuckled against her folds, the vibrations sending delicious ripples straight to her core. Then his mouth was on her clit and when he sucked on the little nub, she shattered around him, the throbbing convulsions racking her body, leaving her trembling and weak. She lay dazed for a moment, surprised that he'd made her orgasm so quickly. The man really knew how to use his mouth.

He crawled up her body and settled his hips between her thighs. "You taste so good, baby." Then, shockingly, he dropped his lips to hers and kissed her deeply. She tasted herself on him, tangy but not at all unpleasant.

"You're still dressed," she mumbled against his mouth.

"True." He planted one last lingering kiss on her lips then slid off the bed.

She leaned back on her elbows and watched as he toed his shoes and socks off and unbuttoned his shirt. The slice of tan firm chest that was revealed to her had her heart rate spiking. He shrugged out of his shirt, undid his jeans and slid them off with his boxers. His cock stood hard and erect against his washboard abdominals and her eyes widened — he was huge. She couldn't stop staring. Something silver glinted at the head of his penis. *What is that?*

He followed her gaze. "It's an apadravya."

"A *what*?"

"Essentially, a cock piercing. It enhances sensation, both yours and mine." He climbed back onto the bed and slid between her thighs, rubbing his cock over her center and dragging it through her folds. She felt the hard, cold metal of the barbell slipping over her moist flesh.

"Ohh," she breathed in appreciation.

He slipped a hand between them and plunged two fingers inside her, curling them and massaging the inner wall of her channel. She stiffened as coils of pleasure spiraled through her.

"That's the spot," he murmured, pumping his fingers in and out of her. She'd thought the G-spot was a load of rubbish—until now. He thrust his fingers deeper, massaging that special area and palming her clit, providing just enough friction. She felt her insides start to tighten.

"Come again, baby. I can feel you're close."

She held her breath and focused on the sensations he was expertly pulling from her. Her legs stiffened and she bucked beneath him, her insides undulating and pulsing as the orgasm ripped through her.

Tanvi lay with her eyes closed, her breath heaving from her exertions. She heard Alexander rummaging in the drawer of the side table. She watched through heavy eyelids as he produced a foil packet and knelt between her thighs. He ripped it open and slid the condom over his substantial erection. *Will he even fit?* It had been far too long since she'd had someone inside her and she didn't think she'd had anyone *that* big.

He resettled himself between her thighs and propped himself on his elbows. "It will fit," he assured her, as if he'd read her mind. "That's why I wanted to prepare you. I needed to make sure you were primed and relaxed. Open your legs wide and bend your knees."

She did as he asked and he dropped his mouth to hers, kissing her deeply. She relaxed beneath him and she gave herself over to his kiss, forcing her tongue into his mouth. She felt the thick head of his cock nudging her entrance and she thrust her hips up. He pushed hard and deep, the sudden, overwhelming invasion bringing tears to her eyes. She felt so full, the stretch slightly painful. He stilled and allowed her to adjust to his size.

"Fuck. You are so tight," he ground out between clenched teeth. "You feel so good. I'm going to move now."

She nodded and swiveled her hips in invitation. He reared back and lunged again deeply, dragging his cock through her folds and using the barbell to exquisite effect. She pumped her hips in time with his thrusts, moaning when he hit a spot deep inside.

Alex plunged again, circling his hips and using his pelvis to rub Tanvi's clit. Her tits bounced and she groaned and writhed beneath him. Her pussy was so hot and tight that he was having trouble maintaining his control. He didn't want to hurt her and it was all he could do to hold back from attacking her like a jackhammer.

He propped himself on his hands and reared back until just the head of his cock nudged her entrance and he held himself there for a moment, breathing deeply. He dropped his gaze between them so he could see where his sheathed cock stretched her wide and a shudder rocked through him. He cupped her ass and rolled over so she was on top of him. He needed to change positions or he was going to lose it.

Tanvi gasped in surprise.

"I need you on top," he grated. "I need you to take control."

He urged her into a sitting position and pulled the tie off the end of her thick braid. He wanted to see her hair out, had dreamed about it.

She ran her hands through her tresses and shook her head. Her glorious hair tumbled around her shoulders in a silken veil.

"Move," he demanded. "You're in charge." He could last as long as he wanted when he wasn't the one in control.

She moved on top of him, circling her hips and riding his cock. Her tits bounced with her movements, her tight little nipples peeking through the veil of her hair. Fuck, she looked so erotic.

He grasped her ankles and bent her knees so her feet were flat on the mattress, spreading her thighs wide. The action revealed her glistening pussy to him, her clit peeking out from under its hood. He thumbed the little nub, massaging and running her juices over the bundle of nerves until he felt Tanvi's insides start to pulse around him, telling him she was close.

He jerked his hips up, bouncing her on top of him. Her channel pulsed and he felt the orgasm overtake her, her internal muscles gripping him impossibly tighter and contracting around his cock, milking him as she shuddered and moaned through her climax.

Alex couldn't wait any longer. He pulled out of her, flipped her onto her hands and knees then grasped her around the waist to force her ass in the air.

She stiffened and he leaned over her back to speak softly in her ear. "I'm going to take you from behind." He caressed her lush ass, reveling in her smooth, silky skin. She relaxed under his touch and backed into his palm. Christ, she was going to be the death of him. He gripped both her hips and lined her up, taking a moment to enjoy the vision she made. She looked so fucking fantastic from that angle, all round hips and ass, her plump breasts bobbing and visible from between her thighs, her ebony hair spread out like a curtain across the crisp white sheets. Yet another moment where he wished he could snap a picture for future reference.

"This is going to be deep. Let me know if it's too much."

He drew back then plunged into her pussy in one swift move, burying himself balls-deep. Tanvi yelped and he leaned forward and whispered in her ear, caressing her butt cheek until he was sure that she was okay. He pulled back and thrust again, spreading her ass cheeks wide so he could see his cock stretching her, her wetness glistening on the root of his dick. *Fuck! That was it!* He moved faster, pulling back then pushing into her hard, yanking her hips toward him to meet his thrusts. He angled his pelvis for the best position, his barbell dragging through her wet folds to flick against her clit. His balls slapped rhythmically against her pussy and desire unfurled then tightened at the base of his spine. Tanvi moaned each time he slammed into her, the head of his cock hitting her cervix.

He felt the trembling in her core. "Don't. Come. Until. I. Say. So," he demanded on each powerful thrust. She whimpered but the pulsations abated a little and he powered on.

His balls tightened and talons of pleasure took hold and raked down his spine. He was going to come and it was going to be massive. He gripped her hips, digging his fingers into her tender flesh and yanking her back onto his solid erection. He gripped the base of the condom, suddenly worried that he would bust the thing off when he shot his load.

"Come," he barked, feeling the tightening deep in her belly. Then she was shattering around him, her channel pulsing and clenching and sending his orgasm bearing down on him like a freight train. He thrust hard and kept his cock buried balls-deep as his climax overtook him, wracking his body with euphoric pleasure.

Chapter Twelve

Tanvi awoke to the feel of silken sheets and a strong arm wrapped around her waist. She stiffened until the last vestiges of sleep cleared and she recalled where she was – in Alexander Banks' bed!

She glanced over her shoulder to where Alexander was still sleeping, his long eyelashes fanned out on his cheeks, giving him a peaceful countenance, at odds with his usually intense demeanor.

She took stock of her body, stretched and winced as a twinge of pain shot between her thighs. It had been a long time since she'd slept with anyone and definitely never anyone as big as Alexander. In fact, she realized that the partners she'd had had not come anywhere near to the sexual prowess that Alexander possessed. Finally, she had a physical term of reference to apply to the alpha male analogy.

She stretched again and felt the tenderness in her breasts where Alexander had kneaded them a little roughly and her nipples were sensitive when they abraded the sheet. She guessed that was what intense fucking was all about and she realized with a jolt that she'd enjoyed it—immensely.

She'd never woken up in a man's bed before and the feeling, while unfamiliar, was also comforting, but perhaps that was just because the man in question was Alexander.

The arm banding around her waist tightened and a low rumbling voice spoke in her ear. "How are you feeling?"

She turned her head to look at him. Hair tousled sexily, his eyelids heavy with the remnants of sleep. He looked—hot.

"I'm fine."

He quirked an eyebrow at her. "Are you being truthful with me? You're not tender at all?"

She looked down. "A little," she finally admitted.

"Good."

Her eyes shot back to his. "Why is that good?"

He shrugged then smirked. "It means you won't forget me in a hurry."

"Hardly," she countered. "I can feel exactly where you've been. It's not as if I could call you gentle." She smirked. "Or small." She didn't know where this feisty, brazen woman had come from, but she liked her.

Alexander frowned, a troubled look crossing his features. "Did I hurt you?"

"No," she said quickly. "I just haven't...experienced anything like that before." In fact, she'd fallen into such a deep and trouble-free sleep after the three incredible orgasms he'd given her that she'd do it all again in a heartbeat. She'd never felt so alive then so relaxed.

He loomed over her suddenly, his muscular chest pressing against her breasts, sending her heart rate hammering. An insistent, heated throbbing strained at her thigh, telling her that he was just as affected by her as she was by him.

Alexander dropped a chaste kiss on her lips. "Come," he murmured against her mouth. "I'll run the shower."

He leaped off the bed and strode toward the bathroom, and Tanvi had the first view of his tight backside and sculpted shoulders. He truly was a magnificent man and she had a difficult time believing that she was in his hotel suite, with him. He stopped and turned around. "Are you coming?"

Her eyes strayed to the impressive erection between his thighs and she couldn't help but be a little in awe of his blatant confidence. She looked up at his smug smile as he stalked back toward the bed.

"You want me to shower with you?"

His smile faltered. "Yes, I'd like you to. But I won't make you do anything you don't want to do."

Tanvi stood, wrapping the sheet around her body. "I've never showered with anyone before."

He arched an eyebrow. "Never?"

She shrugged. "What can I tell you? The occasion just hasn't presented itself before."

He smirked. "Well, you've missed out on a very sensual experience." He grasped her hand and led her to the bathroom. "You know, you'll have to lose the sheet."

"I know. I'm just not accustomed to people seeing me naked." She wasn't shy but a lifetime of covering up and being expected to dress conservatively was a hard habit to break.

Alexander reached into the large shower recess and turned it on. Within moments, steam rose around them.

He collected a number of bath items from a basket on the marble basin.

"In you get," he ordered.

Tanvi dropped the sheet and stepped into the shower recess. There was a bench seat running across one length and it was roomy and luxurious. She'd never seen anything like it.

Alex stepped in behind her and squeezed some shower gel into his palms. He pressed against her back and smoothed his hands over her lower belly, resting his chin on her shoulder. He nipped at her earlobe and nuzzled her throat, keeping his gaze trained on her pert breasts. As he watched, her nipples puckered and lengthened. He palmed them, running the flat of his hands over the stiff little peaks. She moaned and backed into him. Alex bent his knees and nestled his cock between the pillows of her ass. He smoothed a hand down her side and across her hip to dip a finger into her pussy. She was swollen and hot and slick. He added another finger, scissoring them slightly, and pressed a thumb to her clit. She shuddered and groaned. He pushed up higher, massaging the inside wall of her channel and, with his other arm banded around her waist, lifted her off her feet, using the cheeks of her ass to massage his cock as he fingered her.

The water sluiced around them, the fragrant steam rising to mingle with their heavy breathing. She felt so good in his arms, compact, lush and perfect.

She threw her head back to rest on his shoulder and he felt her internal muscles start to quiver. He pulled her tighter against him, rubbing his cock between the cheeks of her ass and pressing on her clit. She stiffened in his arms and groaned as her pussy contracted around his fingers. He held her in place, thrust against her ass twice more and climaxed with a guttural growl, spraying his cum all over her backside. He placed her back on her feet and leaned against the tiled recess, getting his breathing under control.

Alex dropped his head to Tanvi's. "That's one way to wake up in the morning."

She turned around. "I definitely see the appeal of showering together."

He grinned. "Good. Finish up in here and I'll order room service for breakfast."

Chapter Thirteen

Tanvi quickly washed her hair with the shampoo and conditioner provided by the hotel. It was going to take a long time to dry but she didn't think that would matter. It appeared that Alexander wasn't in any hurry to do anything.

She stepped out of the shower and dried herself with a fluffy white bath sheet then tied her hair turban style with a smaller towel. She brushed her teeth and used Alexander's deodorant.

She wandered into the walk-in wardrobe adjoining the bedroom and grabbed a white business shirt, hoping that Alexander wouldn't mind her borrowing it.

When she emerged in the living area, Alexander was taking cloches off a number of room service dishes. He walked toward her and grasped her shoulders. "I like you wearing my shirt. It looks hot." He bent his head and inhaled. "And you smell like me. I like that as well. It appeals to the caveman in me."

Tanvi giggled and waved to the food that was laid out on the dining room table. "I'm starving and the food smells delicious."

"I ordered fruit, scrambled eggs and toast."

She took the chair that Alexander held out for her. "Perfect."

They ate in silence for a while, each lost in their own thoughts until Alexander cleared his throat. "Forgive me if you feel that I'm prying, but you don't seem to be very sexually experienced. Am I right?"

Tanvi eyed him over her cup of tea. "Well, I'm no blushing virgin, but I'm certainly not as experienced as you seem to be."

"I won't deny it." He smirked at her. "But you *can't* deny that it's better for you that I know what I'm doing."

He certainly didn't lack in the self-confidence department, but she had to agree that he'd given her the best sex she'd ever had. "I've only had a few partners. Now I think that they were boys in comparison and they definitely didn't try so hard to please me. In fact, I *had* been wondering what all the fuss was about."

Alexander pushed his chair away from the table and held a hand out to her. "Come here."

Tanvi complied and when she drew close to him, he grasped her hand and pulled her down to straddle his lap. He gripped the bare cheeks of her ass and massaged. "I can tell you haven't had anyone in a while," he murmured. "You're so tight and little. I like that."

She was fast becoming used to his plain talking. Nothing seemed to embarrass him and she found his attitude rubbing off on her and making her less self-conscious.

"Take the towel off your head. I want to see that gorgeous hair."

She pulled the towel off and shook her hair out, the damp tresses raining drops of moisture around them. "Now take a condom from my right pocket."

Tanvi thrust her hand in his pocket and located the foil packet. She popped it between her lips and reached between them to free his cock from his shorts and boxers. It sprang up thick and hard, the silver barbell glinting on the end.

She marveled at the piercing that passed vertically through his glans. "Did it hurt?" she whispered, smoothing her thumb over his tip.

"Yes. But since it healed, the pleasure I now receive is well worth it." He wriggled his eyebrows. "It stimulates me internally, and you internally. The top is positioned to contact your G-spot when I fuck you."

Her nipples pebbled at his crass words. She realized suddenly that she liked it when he talked like that.

"I think it's an Indian word—Sanskrit perhaps?" she mused, still rubbing her thumb over the head of his cock. "I think there was a reference about similar genital piercings in the *Karma Sutra* at one point."

"There's a lot of varying information on the subject," Alexander said through harsh breaths.

She looked up from where she'd been studying his impressive erection. His eyes were closed and his lips were parted, his breathing erratic. She smiled, thrilled to be affecting him so.

She caressed her thumb in circles, applying a little more pressure to his sensitive tip and stimulating white beads of moisture to leak over her fingers.

He pumped his hips and groaned. "Please," he gasped.

She ripped the packet open and rolled the latex down his cock.

He lifted her hips and yanked her down on top of him, thrusting hard and deep. Tanvi threw her head back, gasping as his thick erection pushed through her tender folds.

"Fuck you're tight," he ground between clenched teeth. "Are you too sore?"

"No. I'm good," she breathed.

He gripped her hips and used them to maneuver her, pushing her up then drawing her down and dragging his cock through her folds slowly. He circled his pelvis, grinding into her and sending delicious spirals of pleasure to her core. She threw her arms around his shoulders and dug her nails into his back, bouncing herself on her tiptoes. The position had Alexander thrusting so deeply it was on the verge of painful.

He clutched her hair, winding the thick strands around his wrist and pulling her head down to kiss her roughly. She moaned into his mouth as he slanted his lips across hers and bucked his hips. He tightened his hold on her hair, possessing her with his kiss and tugging until tears gathered in her eyes, the sensuality of the act overcoming any real pain. Her insides quickened and tightened, the telltale pulses in her core gathering momentum.

"You're close," he mumbled against her lips. "I can feel it." He thrust again, bouncing her high on his lap and plunging impossibly deep.

"Oh. That's it!" She shattered around him, her body stiffening then shuddering in release. He followed moments later, holding her tightly and shouting her name as he climaxed.

* * * *

Alex gazed down at where Tanvi was dozing on the sofa. She looked so hot, hair sex-tousled and her lips swollen and ruby red from his rough kissing. She was turning out to be a real little sex kitten — it was definitely taking his business trip to a more enjoyable level. She'd need more stamina, though. He was obviously wearing her out. He'd been pleasantly surprised with her acceptance of a little dominance and she'd seemed to enjoy it. He'd also tested her pain threshold, just a little. A sharp tweak of her nipples, the pulling of her hair, and rather than shirk away from it, she'd appeared to be turned on by it. That was good. He didn't *need* to dominate when he had sex, but there was no denying that was his preference. It was about the trust bestowed by both parties that enhanced the sexual experience. He'd have to try something more serious with her, if she was up for it.

He looked at his watch. It was nearly midday. He'd go down to the lobby shops and see if he could find something for Tanvi.

He draped a light cotton throw over her to ward off the chill of the air conditioning and left the suite. There were a number of shops in the lobby. He remembered a high-end jeweler, lingerie store, boutique, a carpet gallery and a few others. He'd be able to get what he wanted in one of them.

* * * *

Tanvi awoke curled up on the sofa. She was surprised at how much and how well she'd been sleeping. Usually her slumber was troubled and sporadic, but today she felt refreshed. There was obviously something to be said for lots of good sex and throwing her worries to the wind.

The suite door opened and Alexander walked inside, his arms full of bags.

Tanvi sat up, a little embarrassed that she'd fallen asleep so quickly after waking up that morning. "I'm sorry," she murmured. "I must have been tired."

He dropped the bags on the floor and sat next to her on the sofa. "Don't apologize. I've worn you out. You're not used to this level of…activity."

She smirked at him. "That's an understatement. What did you buy?"

"Things for you."

She raised her eyebrows. "I don't need anything."

"Have a look. I want to go sightseeing with you and I know you didn't bring a change of clothes."

No, she hadn't wanted to seem too forward. She smiled and took the bags from him. "Thank you. That's very thoughtful."

She wandered into the bedroom and opened the bags. Inside the first there was champagne-colored satin and lace lingerie—boy pants and a demi bra. Another produced a brightly colored *kurta*, matching shawl and plain cotton *churidars*. It was perfect, just what she would have chosen for herself.

She changed quickly and was surprised to find that the lingerie fit her. She didn't dwell on how Alexander had become so good at estimating a woman's size. She wrapped her long hair into a high topknot and applied some light makeup from the small makeup purse that she kept in her handbag. She slipped on her sandals and was ready.

Chapter Fourteen

When Tanvi stepped out of the bedroom, Alex applauded himself on his choice of outfit. He'd had advice from the shop assistant, but the ultimate choice had been his. Tanvi looked stunning. The *kurta* fit her perfectly and enhanced her lush breasts and small waist and the *churidars* emphasized her slim calves. He'd toyed with the idea of purchasing something a little more Western but had decided that it might draw more attention her way and something told him that she was keen to avoid recognition.

She fished a pair of large, dark sunglasses out of her handbag. They suited her but also succeeded in covering half of her face — another indicator that she didn't want to be recognized. He wondered briefly who would identify her easily in such a populated city, but it was obviously something that concerned her.

Alex held his hand out to her. "You look gorgeous."

"Thank you. I approve of your choices."

"There was something in those bags that I believe I purchased with only myself in mind." He gave her a pointed look and was gratified when she blushed. "Where do you suggest we start with the sightseeing?"

"We could visit the Red Fort then the Qutub Minar and perhaps finish at Khan Market." She gave him an impish smile. "There are some decent restaurants there, but I also saw a pair of shoes that I've decided I have to have."

He grinned. "Women and shoes. It's good to know it's the same the world over."

She giggled. "If a girl wants a nice pair of bling sandals, Khan Market is where we go."

Alex grasped her hand. "I'll call Sanjay on the way down to the lobby."

* * * *

Tanvi had had an enjoyable day with Alexander. She'd been able to give him quite a bit of history regarding the sites they'd visited, and Alexander had impressed her with his attentiveness and the questions he'd asked. He was obviously very interested in the historical aspects of her city and the realization endeared him to her further.

Now they were sitting in a restaurant in Khan Market drinking a ludicrously priced cocktail and sharing a plate of kebabs with chutney.

"So this market is one of the priciest retail areas in India?" Alexander asked, gazing out of the window, his expression dubious.

"Yes, apparently." Tanvi peered out at the streetscape and could forgive Alexander his uncertainty. When she saw the market through his eyes, she couldn't miss the numerous stray dogs, potholes filled with water and the odd cow. At first glance it definitely didn't rate up among the rich retail areas of America that she'd seen. "Well, it's India's version," she amended.

They shared a look across the table then both erupted into laughter.

"It's one of the things I love about India," Alex said. "It's so vibrant and colorful and nothing is ever as one would expect."

"That's true," Tanvi agreed. "With a population as big and as culturally diverse as ours, you learn to always expect the unexpected. It's quite different from the West." She studied him across the table, trying to formulate her next question. "I assume you don't have a girlfriend?" She'd attempted for casual but wasn't sure she'd pulled it off.

"I don't have someone special, no."

She gave him an arch look. "What does that mean?"

"It means that I see some women from time to time but no one exclusively."

What? Does that mean that I'm one of many? A cold sliver of dread worked its way down her spine. She shouldn't be worried by his answer. Neither of them had indicated that what they were doing was anything more than a quick fling, and she had no business feeling disappointed. The emotion was there, nevertheless.

"Oh." She shrugged. She didn't want him thinking that his answer bothered her. In fact, the realization that it *did* bother her left her feeling uneasy and suddenly in very unfamiliar territory. She was immensely relieved when Alex changed the subject.

"What do you like to do? What are your hobbies?"

"I do yoga and Bollywood dancing. I enjoy reading and cooking and once a week I volunteer at an orphanage."

"I can see you volunteering at an orphanage. What do you do there?"

"Anything they need, but mainly I read to the children, teach them English and sometimes I help in the kitchen." She smiled. "I also like helping with the babies."

The way Tanvi's eyes shone when she spoke about the children told Alex that she cared deeply about them. He determined there and then that he wanted to help. "I'd like to go with you one day."

Her eyes widened in surprise then a beautiful grin lit up her face. "Of course. The children would love that. I'll let you know next time I go in."

"You also mentioned Bollywood dancing?" That intrigued him. He didn't know much about it, but he imagined that Tanvi looked fantastic doing it.

"Yes. I love it! Riya and I do it together. It's great fun and excellent exercise. What about you?" Tanvi asked. "What do you like to do?"

"I swim, I do weights and I box. I also have some" — he waved his hand in the air vaguely — "other activities that I enjoy." He would tell Tanvi about his BDSM predilection, but now was not the time or the place and he was relieved when she didn't pursue his ambiguous answer. He looked at his watch. In fact, perhaps the time to test those waters was fast approaching.

He waved over the waiter and asked for the bill.

Chapter Fifteen

Tanvi agreed to spend another night with Alex. Well, he hadn't asked, just assumed that she was going to. Strangely, she wasn't bothered by his rather high-handed attitude but found herself going along with it. Besides, she'd much prefer to spend the evening with Alex in his sumptuous hotel room than at home, listening to her father nag her — there really wasn't a decision to make in her mind. She'd simply told her parents that she was staying with a friend. She often did that so it wouldn't cause any awkward questions.

Alex opened the door of his suite and ushered her inside. "I want you to undress but leave your lingerie on, then lie on the bed."

A tingling of anticipation rippled down Tanvi's spine as she hurried into the bedroom. She loved that he was so dominant. She didn't have to think about anything, didn't have to second-guess herself. It was so easy to give herself over to Alex. She paused. *When did I start thinking of him as Alex instead of Alexander?* When had she subconsciously crossed the line into friend territory? She shook her head. It didn't matter. In fact, informality seemed more natural somehow.

She undressed quickly and surveyed herself in the mirror. The lingerie was perfect for her body type. The boy pants cut high up her backside but flattered her hips and waist and the demi bra lifted her breasts, the cups so low her areolae peeked over the tops. She untied her hair from its topknot and ran a brush through the thick strands.

A flush spread over her skin as she lay on the bed. Music filtered in from the living area. It was haunting and beautiful and sensual. A shiver shot through her, peaking her nipples into tight points. She tried to relax and let the music wash over her, but anxious tension gripped her. There was something about Alex's demeanor that had changed. It was only subtle, but it was there glinting in his eyes and a harsher note to his tone. It was also the music putting her on edge. It promised something…more.

She heard Alexander come in and approach the bed — well, not heard him exactly — but felt his presence, an elusive change in the atmosphere and a slight woodsy scent. She held her breath, eyes closed and waited.

His hand on her thigh made her jump. A soft caress as he smoothed his large palm over her knee and down her calf.

"You are so beautiful. Lying there like a decadent dessert. A vision in champagne lace just for me."

His deep voice rolled over her and she relaxed under his touch.

"You may open your eyes."

She blinked, trying to adjust to the dim light. Alex stood next to the bed dressed in nothing but jeans. His powerful chest, hard and defined, his abdominal muscles sculpted and lean—like a Greek god. He took her breath away.

"Do you trust me?" he asked, his voice low, but his tone audible over the music.

She realized suddenly that she did. Whatever he was going to do to her—she wanted it. Instinctively, she knew that he wouldn't hurt her.

"Yes," she breathed. The song continued its lilting, haunting melody. "What's the music?"

"It's FKA Twigs, her *EP2*. Do you like it?"

"I do. It's quite moving."

He chuckled and grasped her foot. "That's not the adjective I was aiming for. I prefer erotic." He dug his thumbs into her arch, sending a sharp sensation shooting to her sex. She groaned and writhed.

"Keep still," he demanded. "Absorb it."

She stilled and sucked in a breath, focusing on the unfamiliar feelings he was provoking within her.

He produced a purple scarf. "I'm going to blindfold you. It will heighten your perception of touch and sound."

She nodded and Alex tied it around her head, cutting off her vision. He was right, almost immediately her perception of the music intensified, as did her awareness of him. She sensed him moving, felt the light draft as he walked out of her periphery. Then she heard the clinking of...chains? She stiffened. *What is he going to do?*

"Relax, sweetness. I'm not going to hurt you." He was back beside her, sweeping his palm up and down her thigh, calming her.

"You need to tell me if anything I do makes you uncomfortable. These sensations can be...intense.

Think of a word to use if you want me to stop. A safe word."

Her breath hitched and her pulse thrummed in excitement.

"Kismet."

"Interesting choice. Why that word?"

She gave a little shrug. "It seems fitting, I guess."

"You expected to find someone who was into BDSM?" His tone was one of surprise.

"No, destiny brought me to you."

"Hmm, well I hope you never have to use it," he murmured, caressing her thigh a moment longer, soothing her. "I'm going to handcuff you to the bed now."

Tanvi's heart rate ratcheted as he took each of her wrists and locked them into the cuffs so her arms were raised above her head, manacled to the bars of the bed head. They were softer than she imagined, fur lined. She relaxed a little, the music swirling around her, and Alex's presence, steady and strong, calming her.

"Remember that this is for pleasure. Focus on what I'm doing to you."

Something light and soft, like a feather, brushed her flesh. Alex tickled her with it a moment, making her squirm.

"Keep still or I'll cuff your ankles."

She breathed deeply and focused on the sensations, maintaining steady breathing as her senses were assailed and tormented. Starting at her left clavicle, he brushed the plume over her shoulder, down her arm to her wrist, swirling it over the top of her hand then down each finger. The feathery caresses stopped for a moment, then he was touching her breasts, kneading her flesh and pinching her nipples through the rough lace of her bra. She moaned and arched her back, pushing her breasts more firmly into his palms.

"You like that," he murmured. Then, after yanking the cups of her bra down, he sucked hard on each nipple, sparking a sharp quivering at her core.

She gasped and groaned, trying desperately to stay still.

He blew on the tips, his breath elongating them to painfully hard peaks.

"That…is…so…hot," he whispered. "You should see your breasts now, so plump and swollen by your desire and wet from my mouth. Your tight little buds are so erect and rosy. I want to chew on them."

"Please, I want you to." She wanted it desperately. She wanted him everywhere—needed it. Moisture pooled in her pussy and she was glad of her panties. The anticipation had her aching inside, had her sex throbbing with need.

She felt his warm breath coast over one nipple, then he was sucking and nibbling on the stiff peak. She gasped as lightning bolts of pleasure-pain sizzled through her and landed between her thighs.

He took her other taut bud into his mouth, drawing on it with long, hard pulls and pinching the other between thumb and forefinger.

"Oh, God." She gulped. Pleasure coiled and coalesced deep inside, tightening and gathering momentum. "I'm going to come."

He sucked harder, exerting a little more pressure, and she shattered. Pulses of pleasure undulated her core, leaving her trembling and dazed and *surprised*.

"You are perfect," Alex murmured. "So responsive to my touch."

She felt his hands at her back, unclasping her bra and pushing it up her arms to her bound wrists. Then he was pulling her panties down her legs, grasping each ankle and spreading her thighs, leaving her bare and exposed.

"You are so wet. I can see your juices glistening on that sweet pussy." He swiped a finger up her center and massaged her clit. She arched off the bed, desperate for more. Her first orgasm had left her mildly unsatisfied and the throbbing had returned. *What is he doing to me?*

"You need something more," Alex voiced her thoughts. A light caress touched her inner thigh – the feather. He swirled it in circles for a moment, then he slowly drew it up to tickle and tease her pussy. "You're tight with nervous tension and you want my cock filling you."

"Yes!" The throbbing had grown to painful proportions and she needed a release.

He teased her with the feather, inexorably running it across her pussy lips, swirling it through her moisture and tormenting her relentlessly.

"Please," she begged, bowing off the bed and pushing herself toward him.

"Soon," he crooned, his voice low at her ear.

She heard a click then an odd buzzing. *What is that?*

Alex answered her unspoken question. "This is a clitoral vibrator. It's new. I purchased it before I left Australia. You're so wet we won't need lube."

He grasped her ankles and spread her legs wide. Something hard and cold brushed across her clit, vibrating against the bundle of nerves. She jumped in surprise as pleasure streaked through her.

"Ohhh," she groaned and thrust her hips up. Sensation swirled and coalesced at her core, tightening her insides.

Alex thrust two fingers into her channel and caressed her inner wall, high and deep, keeping the vibrator pulsing on her sensitive clit.

"That's it. You're fluttering around my fingers."

She held her breath, her legs going rigid as the pleasure mounted. Her inner muscles clenched and pulsed and the climax ripped through her. Alex kept her legs spread wide and the vibe on her tingling clit, spurring her orgasm to go and on, leaving her weak and breathless.

Tanvi slumped on the bed, perspiration dotting her forehead. She was absolutely exhausted. She knew now why Alex wanted her to have a safe word. The sensations he aroused in her were extremely intense, sometimes almost painfully so.

She felt his cock at her mouth. He was running the head over her lips, smearing his pre-cum like erotic lipstick. The musky scent of him was strong and masculine, his taste slightly salty. She licked the head of his cock, teasing his barbell piercing with her tongue and stretching her lips over his swollen crown.

He groaned and pumped his hips, gripping her hair in a fist and manipulating her head, forcing his cock deeper into her throat.

She relaxed her jaw and swallowed him, reveling in his musky taste, her lips wide toward his base. She couldn't take all of him—he was too big—but she'd take what she could.

Alex pressed a button on the iPod docking station control and changed the music, choosing *Closer* by Nine

Inch Nails. He wanted to ramp up the mood. He needed something appropriate for hard fucking.

Christ, Tanvi looked so hot and erotic with his cock in her mouth, plump lips strained over the thick head, a purple blindfold obscuring her vision and her hair sexily disheveled, tumbling around her head like black molasses. He pumped his hips and fucked her mouth, her saliva and his pre-cum easing his glide. Her lips were shiny and swollen from the strain of taking his cock and he had to work hard not to blow his load down her throat at the sheer eroticism of it. His balls tightened and lust coiled at the base of his spine. He was close but he wanted to come inside her.

He pulled out of her mouth with a wet pop and grabbed a condom from the side table. He had a vague thought that perhaps his choice of song was a little *too* much. Then sensation overtook him. He sheathed himself quickly—keen to get between those gorgeous thighs and into that tight wet pussy.

He settled between her legs and dropped his mouth to hers. She smelled of his cum and it was so fucking hot. He wanted to taste himself on her. He took her lips in a sensual kiss, sweeping his tongue through her mouth, savoring the flavor of her mixed with him. He ground his hips against her pelvis, dragging his sheathed cock through her pussy lips and using his apadravya to stimulate her clit. She groaned into his mouth.

"Are you sensitive?" he mumbled against her lips.

"Yes."

"Good." He grunted, reared back then slammed into her in one hard thrust.

She cried out and shuddered, her pussy clenching around his cock like a fist. He started to move, setting his thrusts to the rhythm of the music and hitting her high and deep.

She moaned beneath him, her blindfold ensuring that all her perceptions were enhanced. He pulled out and pumped in, dragging the head of his cock through her folds and hitting the sensitive nerve endings. Her insides quivered and pulsed. Thank fuck—he didn't think he could hold out much longer.

She stiffened and screamed into his mouth as the orgasm overtook her.

He quickened his pace, drawing out all the way before slamming back into her tight, wet heat. His balls pulled up and lust tightened the base of his spine and he pumped harder. Sweat broke out on his brow and he held his breath as he surged home, thrusting twice and burying himself balls-deep, coming inside her.

Chapter Sixteen

Tanvi had had a perfect weekend. There was something about Alexander that had her acting all shivery and excited like a schoolgirl. She enjoyed spending time with him and had avoided dwelling on the fact that it couldn't last. She'd determined to relish their time together while she had it and she'd make the most of it. Never had she experienced such intense sexual responses. No man before Alex had even been successful in giving her an orgasm—now she'd experienced three in a row! He'd ruined her for other men, of that she was certain, but she wouldn't regret a moment of it.

What was that quote by Tennyson? 'Tis better to have loved and lost than never to have loved at all.' Then it hit her—realization slamming into her chest—she was falling for him!

An email message prompted her out of her reverie. It was from Alex, the subject title intriguing her—BDSM Submissive Guide.

She smiled, opened it and started to read. She was pleased to discover nothing totally shocking to her. It was exactly like what she'd read about, what she wanted. She couldn't say precisely why. Perhaps it was because it was *her* choice.

She would be the one to decide what she wanted and how she wanted it and with whom. There was something about a dominant male that called to her, that stirred something deep in her belly.

But she didn't want the nasty, chauvinistic dominance that Rakesh would be capable of. That sort of dominance was for men who were insecure and weak, men who needed to exert control in order to make up for their perceived inadequacies. It wasn't the same as the mutual trust and understanding that she believed made up a D/s relationship. From what she understood, the submissive in the union was actually the one who held the power, who had the control to stop and influence the Dominant.

An hour later, she was still trawling through the Internet BDSM sites and reading everything she could about the scene, as Alex had termed it in his email to her. She wondered why he hadn't spoken to her about his BDSM preferences but had chosen instead to write to her about it? Perhaps he wanted to give her time to digest the information. After all, it wasn't every day that someone told her they were into BDSM.

She sat back in her desk chair as she thought about what she'd just learned. Alex was a Dominant. She wasn't surprised since he had dominant alpha male written all over him.

Tanvi comprehended suddenly that she'd been acting like a submissive with Alex, that he'd been exerting a dominance over her and she'd been subconsciously obeying him. Would he hurt her? Did he want to hit her with a whip or paddle or flogger? She thought about it for a moment and there was no escaping the fact that she trusted Alex. She'd allow him to do those things to her because she was intrigued — she wanted to test her limits.

The buzzing of her desk phone jerked her out of her thoughts. She answered it. It was reception telling her that she had a visitor — her uncle.

* * * *

Alex had worked in his suite all morning, checking emails and going through some company portfolios. He'd decided to head down to the hotel bar for a sandwich and use the break to catch up on the news.

He strolled into the lobby and stopped dead in his tracks when he saw Tanvi with an older gentleman. The man was grasping her arm and was talking urgently to her in Hindi, occasionally shaking her.

Anger hit him square in the gut at the man mistreating her. *Who the fuck is he? And why does he have his hands on her?*

Alex stalked toward them. The man jerked his head up as Alex approached, anger clear on his features. He said a few more parting words, which Alex didn't understand, dropped Tanvi's arm and spun on his heel.

As Alex drew level with her, he could see that she was shaking.

"Who the fuck was that?" he demanded a little too harshly, making her jump.

She turned around to face him. "My uncle." She waved a hand in the air. "He's a little…upset with me about something."

"What?"

"It's nothing that you need to worry about. A family matter."

Alex studied her, unconvinced, but decided not to push it. He took her hand and drew her toward a private corner. "Are you free this evening?"

"No. I have plans."

Alex gave her a hard look. He hadn't expected her to be busy and it pissed him off, more than it should.

"Well, have you had lunch? I'm going to the bar for a sandwich. I'd like you to join me." He toyed with the idea of ordering her to, but thought better of it. That sort of approach required more discussion. He was sure she'd make an excellent submissive, had proven so far that she would, but, up until now, he didn't think that she was aware of what she'd been doing. It was an instinctive thing with her, to allow him to dominate, but whether she'd be so compliant when she understood exactly what was going on and that there was a term for what they were doing, a label — he didn't know.

Eventually, she nodded and he led her to the lobby bar. They each ordered and he waited for the waiter to leave before broaching the subject uppermost in his mind.

"I assume you received my email?"

She fidgeted and looked away. "I did but I'm not sure that this is an appropriate place for that sort of conversation."

He chuckled and glanced around the bar. There were a couple of tables with customers, but none of them were paying any attention to him and Tanvi. "No one is listening to us. I think you're just delaying the inevitable."

She sighed. "You're right. I'm just not sure what it is you want from me. What is this" — she waved a hand in the air — "that we're doing? Do you want a short-term D/s relationship? Is that even possible?"

He spluttered on his water, her response taking him totally off guard. She'd either done a hell of a lot of research since this morning, or she had some prior understanding of BDSM and its various elements.

It was a damn good question and he told her so. He took a sip of his water and a moment to think about the best way to respond. The waiter arrived with their club sandwiches, giving him a little longer to formulate what he wanted to say.

"I enjoy your company, Tanvi. I think we're good together. We have chemistry. I can't tell you exactly how long I plan to stay here but I'd like to explore things further with you." He shrugged. "I'd like to introduce you to some aspects but only if you're completely willing and comfortable." He leaned toward her and lowered his voice. "We'll just spice things up a little, sweetness. We can continue to fuck each other's brains out, at least while I'm here." He wasn't sure why he added that last bit. But he couldn't promise anything else and he didn't want to give her the wrong idea.

She picked at her lunch, nibbling on a small triangle of her club. She placed her sandwich back on the plate and pushed it aside. "Is this what you usually do? Find a woman at each of your business destinations and have a short-lived fling with them?"

Alex reached across the table and clasped her hand. "I deserved that. I suppose I didn't express myself particularly well."

"No. You were quite clear. I appreciate your honesty. As it happens, what you're suggesting works for me too."

He should have felt relieved, but an inexplicable frisson of anger rippled down his spine. He tamped down the sensation. He was acting like a hypocritical ass.

Alex set his features into an impassive mask. "Good. Then we're on the same page. You obviously have some knowledge and understanding about the different aspects of BDSM?"

"Not first-hand. Only what I've read."

He was relieved by her answer, more than he cared to admit. For reasons he didn't want to analyze, he was pleased that she didn't have any previous experience.

"I'm intrigued." She blushed and looked down at the table. "And excited."

His cock swelled and pushed against his zipper. Fuck, he couldn't wait to get her alone again. "You said you were busy this evening?"

She nodded, diverting her eyes. *What isn't she telling me?* He assessed her for a moment but decided not to push it. It was none of his business after all.

"Fine," he eventually capitulated. "Keep the following evening free."

She looked at her watch. "I have to go. I'll see you tomorrow."

"I'll text you the details," he promised, rising and pulling her chair out for her.

She gave him a small smile and placed her hand on his arm. "Thank you for lunch."

Alex watched her leave, an odd foreboding twisting his gut. He shook his head, surprised at his reaction. There was something about Tanvi that intrigued and fascinated him. He couldn't deny the attraction he felt for her, and her easy compliance regarding their *fling*, as she'd termed it, irritated him. He couldn't fathom why. It was what he wanted after all. Wasn't it?

Chapter Seventeen

Tanvi applied the finishing touches to her makeup. She dusted her lids with pewter-blue shadow and lined her eyes with black kohl. She'd decided on a navy blue saree with flecks of silver. A dark color to reflect her mood – somber.

Her uncle had bullied her into attending the function that evening with Rakesh. He'd threatened all sorts of repercussive actions if she didn't go. She was playing a dangerous game. She knew if her uncle discovered her relationship with Alex, there'd be hell to pay. But she'd agreed to attend to keep the peace *and* so as not to raise suspicions. She was determined to get as much out of her short time with Alex as she could and she didn't want to do anything to jeopardize that. Never had she felt so euphoric and free as she did when she was with him. He did things to her that no other man had ever done, made her feel like no other man had ever made her feel. Why would she give that up sooner than she had to?

She hadn't formally agreed to a marriage with Rakesh. Her family had assumed that the match they had chosen for her would go ahead. She was expected to obey their wishes, be thankful even that they had been so considerate and careful in their selection. She sighed heavily. Perhaps she should give Rakesh a chance. After all, there would be no knight in shining armor riding to her rescue. Her fate was sealed, so she may as well try to make the situation better for herself. While Alex was a pleasant diversion, he was just that — a diversion — there could be no future for them and Alex didn't want that at any rate.

"Tanvi!" her mother called. "The driver is here."

She checked her reflection one last time and picked up her small evening bag.

To her surprise, Rakesh was waiting for her by the open back door of the car. She allowed him to assist her into the back seat. It was very out of character for Rakesh. The few times she'd been in his presence, he'd shown no interest in acting remotely courteous.

He grasped her hand. "How are you, Tanvi?"

She shot him a wary look. "I'm well, thank you." Although she wasn't well, she was suddenly feeling a little nervous. This side of Rakesh was alien to her and she wasn't sure how to react.

"You look beautiful. That color suits you," he murmured, using his thumb to draw circles on the top of her hand.

She smiled weakly and willed herself to remain calm. Something wasn't right. Rakesh had never been this attentive. In fact she could only ever recall a few words that he'd actually spoken to her.

They arrived at the function center. A long line of vehicles snaked ahead of them and flashes from cameras flared brightly as cars stopped to deposit their passengers. Finally, it was their turn to alight, and a liveried young man marched forward to open her door. Tanvi stepped gracefully from the vehicle and right into Rakesh, who'd made it to her side in record time. A red carpet stretched before them, cameramen jostling to take their photo as they walked up to the entrance. They drew closer to the doors and Tanvi moved subtly to the side, trying to put a discreet distance between herself and Rakesh.

"Not so fast," he whispered harshly in her ear and wrapped an arm around her waist, digging his fingers into her hip painfully. "You're here with me. You'll have your photo taken with me and you'll smile about it!" His tone was low and cold and sent a shiver of apprehension rippling through her.

Tanvi looked toward the cameramen and managed a halfhearted smile, trying not to wince as Rakesh dug his fingers into her sensitive flesh.

"That's a good girl," he murmured when the flashes finally subsided. He gripped her hand and walked through the doors, pulling her behind him.

As soon as they entered, Tanvi spotted her uncle across the room talking to some men. Her chest tightened in alarm. She'd never been close to her uncle, had even feared him a little. When she was growing up, he'd always been distant and had kept her at arm's length. She wasn't sure if his having no children had made it difficult for him to relate or if he just wasn't a particularly warm man—she suspected the latter. Seeing him now made her edgy. The charity function wasn't something that he would usually attend and she suspected that he did so this evening for a particular reason. Her uneasiness grew when she considered Rakesh's odd behavior.

Her uncle caught her eye and made his way toward them. "Good, you made it," he said by way of a greeting. "It's time," he continued, "that you make this unofficial arrangement official."

Tanvi gaped at him, a cold feeling of dread flooding her veins. Apparently her fling with Alex would be ending sooner than either of them had anticipated.

* * * *

Alex stalked into the Totally Five Star lobby. He'd had a long day involved in meetings and was knee-deep in paperwork. He wanted nothing more than a cold beer and a shower. He might even skip his workout, which was unlike him, but he just didn't feel up to it.

All day his mind had been continually drawn to Tanvi. He had an insidious feeling that her inability to meet him had something to do with another man. It had been her evasive demeanor that had raised his suspicions. He told himself that he had no right to doubt her and no right to question her whereabouts, but he couldn't help it and the unfamiliar feelings were disturbing his equilibrium. In the past, he'd had no qualms about the women in his life playing the field, provided that they were honest about it. Now Tanvi had entered his sphere of existence and he suddenly felt protective, jealous even—emotions that had been otherwise alien to him.

As he was approaching reception, one of the staff members caught his eye and beckoned him over.

"Mr. Banks, sir, you have a visitor. I requested that they wait in the lobby bar for you."

A visitor? Who the hell would be visiting me? He walked to the bar, scanning the crowd for a familiar face when he saw something all *too* familiar, visible above the back of a chair, an unmistakable head of fiery red curls!

What the fuck? He rounded the chair cautiously and his suspicions were confirmed.

"Alex, darling. I've been waiting for you for an age."

"Marla," he muttered, remembering too late the message he'd left on her phone days ago.

"Is that any way to greet me?" she remonstrated playfully as she stood and wrapped her arms around his neck. "It's good to see you, handsome."

Alex returned her hug briefly and placed a quick kiss on the cheek she offered him. He couldn't help feeling like he was embracing a bag of bones. Placing his hands on her shoulders he urged her to arm's length in a gesture meant to look like he was appraising her. "You look great," he murmured for good measure.

She smiled coquettishly. "Thank you."

She'd sheathed her willowy frame in a designer linen suit, her sky-high heels bringing her almost to his height. Where once he'd admired her model-thin physique, now he only saw a figure too lean and angular. He realized with a jolt that he felt none of the familiar stirrings of lust. She was just an attractive woman with whom he'd spent time in the past. Sure, she was into the BDSM scene and they'd had some mind-blowing times together, but even the possibility of some kinky sex didn't get his juices flowing.

What the hell do I do now? He cleared his throat and took a seat in the chair opposite hers. "I didn't realize you were coming."

Marla sat and picked up her glass of champagne, a frown marring her perfect features. "I wanted to surprise you, but you don't seem particularly happy to see me, Alex."

For a brief, vengeful moment, he wondered about taking her up to his suite, then his better instincts cut in. He had no idea what Tanvi was actually doing, and bedding Marla out of misplaced spite would be a deplorable act, for all concerned.

He gave her a tight smile. "I just expected you to call."

She smiled slyly, uncrossed her legs and stroked her right foot up to his thigh. "Well, I'm here now, handsome. I was actually in the Maldives for a shoot when I got your message so it really couldn't have worked out better."

Alex's mind whirled. *Should I just tell Marla that there's someone else?* But he and Tanvi had nothing serious. They'd discussed their agreement for a short-term affair, no strings attached, which is exactly the type of relationship he had with Marla. If he blew Marla off now, she'd be pissed and he'd no doubt be jeopardizing any future hookups with her. But what other option was there? He definitely wouldn't be fucking Marla's brains out the one evening Tanvi couldn't be with him. He decided that telling Marla the truth was the only decent option.

Alex glanced across at her. She'd undone her jacket to reveal a pink camisole, her little, braless nipples jutting against the soft fabric. She leaned forward in an obvious display of flirtatious enticement and he wasn't the least bit interested. Her breasts were virtually nonexistent and definitely not in the league of Tanvi's plump, luscious rack. He recalled the feel of Tanvi's breasts in his palms, heavy and succulent as he pinched her perky nipples, and he had to shift in his seat, his cock swelling hard and insistent at the memory.

Unfortunately, Marla didn't miss the bulge at his crotch. "Ah," she breathed lustily. "There's my big boy."

He arranged his features into an impassive mask, deciding that he had to take action and cut her off, sooner rather than later. "Marla, I'm sorry that you've diverted here. I forgot that I left that message for you. I wish you'd called me before deciding to change your plans."

She sat back in her chair, her gaze narrowing. "What are you talking about?"

Alex sighed and shoved his hands through his hair. He hated to do this to her, but he could see no other way. *Why the fuck did I leave that message?* "I've met someone," he said quietly. "She lives here in New Delhi."

"And you're obviously fucking her," Marla snarled, her cheeks flushing an angry red.

Alex's jaw tensed. "That's none of your business."

"Of course you are," she scoffed. "When have you ever been able to keep it in your pants? You can't go a week without calling on a woman to ease your rampant sexual appetites."

"Perhaps," he conceded with a nonchalant shrug. "But you *know* the deal, Marla. What we do" — he waved a hand between them — "is nothing but casual and strictly no strings attached. We fuck, then we go our separate ways. It's always been like that, through mutual agreement until one of us changes it. I'm changing it. I apologize for your inconvenience but nothing can happen now."

Marla's eyes flashed. "You're an ass," she hissed.

"I'm sorry." He shrugged. "I'll give you the money for your flight and pay for a room here for you until you can change your plans."

She stood quickly. "Don't bother. I'm going straight to the airport." She grabbed her handbag and small suitcase.

"I'm sorry," he repeated, not sure what else he could say to her.

She ignored him, turned and strode to the exit.

Alex watched her go, surprised that he had no feelings of regret, only that Marla had been troubled by his failure to rectify the situation before she'd arrived. He was thankful that Tanvi had had other plans. The two women meeting could have been a very awkward situation indeed.

Chapter Eighteen

Tanvi hadn't slept well, she'd tossed and turned for the most of the night, thinking over what her uncle had said the previous evening. Obviously his plans for her were high on his list of priorities. She didn't have too much time or freedom left.

She arrived at the Totally Five Star a little late and went straight to her office, determined to catch up on the invoices that had been gathering on her desk. She booted up her computer and checked her mobile for messages. There were two. One from Alex, and the other from her friend Riya. She was about to respond when her phone vibrated with an incoming call.

"Hello."

"Oh, my God, Tanvi. I have to talk to you," Riya breathed down the phone.

"What's wrong?"

"I have to tell you what I saw last night. You'll never believe it!"

* * * *

Alex had left three text messages with Tanvi and she'd answered none of them. He'd decided to head back to the hotel at lunchtime to track her down. She was either busy, or she was avoiding him and it had better not fucking be the latter.

He strode through the lobby toward the administration offices at the back. He arrived at Tanvi's door, rapped once and stalked through.

She jumped when he entered then swiveled her chair around to face him.

"Have you been too busy to answer my messages?" He tried to keep his voice even, but he couldn't help a note of irritation creeping in.

She regarded him steadily. "I have been busy, yes. But that's not the reason that I haven't responded to you."

"Well, please enlighten me," he drawled sarcastically.

"Riya called me this morning. You remember my friend Riya?"

Alex nodded once brusquely, wondering where she was going with this line of conversation.

"She saw you yesterday evening at the bar. She'd just finished a yoga class and was walking through the lobby. She told me that you were with a woman and that you two looked to be very close."

Ah, now the reason for her evasion was clear, although jumping so quickly to the wrong conclusions would earn her a punishment later. He grew solid just thinking about the things he would do to her then gave himself a mental shake. Now was not the time to get a roaring hard-on.

"That woman, Marla, is just a friend."

Tanvi raised her eyebrows at him. "She was stroking your thigh with her foot. Do all your friends do that?"

He huffed in frustration. "No. She *is* a friend, but we've...had relations in the past."

Her eyes grew wide with surprise. "Relations?"

He clenched his jaw. "Fine. You want me to spell it out. We used to fuck each other, okay?"

Tanvi gasped. "So that's why she was here? Riya told me she had luggage with her. Was she planning on spending the night, or perhaps a few days? So you could take up where you left off?"

He cursed softly. "It wasn't like that. At the beginning of my stay here, I left a message on her phone, telling her where I was. I hadn't even met you at that stage and I completely forgot that I'd left the message. But I'm telling you that nothing happened. In fact, she was very pissed off when I informed her that my situation had changed. She stormed out."

He stepped toward Tanvi and grasped her hand, pulling her out of her chair and into his arms. "I'm being totally honest with you," he murmured, looking down into her face and stroking her jaw with his thumb. "

Tanvi gazed up at him, indecision warring within her. She'd been shocked then angry when she'd spoken to Riya earlier that morning. But Alex's explanation did sound reasonable. According to Riya, the woman had looked like a model, tall and very slim with fiery red hair. No doubt Tanvi would have heard from the staff about such a stunning woman staying at the hotel.

"Who is she?" she eventually asked.

"Just someone I see from time to time. She's a model so her photo-shoots take her around the globe. Often she's in a similar part of the world as I am. I know it sounds bad, but we have a no-strings-attached relationship. It works for both of us." Alex gave her a crooked grin. "Well, it did until now. And I have to say that seeing her again did nothing for me."

"Riya said that she's very beautiful."

He shrugged. "I thought so at one time." He smoothed his palms down her sides and grasped her ass cheeks. "But I've since met a woman who I think is far more beautiful, smart, sexy" — he gave her backside a squeeze — "and deliciously voluptuous."

Tanvi gasped and leaned closer to him, squashing her breasts against his hard chest.

Alex dropped his head to hers. "Where's George?" he whispered, his warm breath tickling her ear.

"He's not coming in today."

Alex released her and locked the office door. He stalked over to the desk, swiped all the paperwork onto the floor, lifted her around the waist and deposited her on the desktop.

"Alex! We can't," Tanvi cried in horror when she realized his intentions.

"Be quiet," he ordered, his voice low and rough. He produced a clean handkerchief from his pocket and urged it into her mouth. "Bite down on this if you need to." He smirked. "Besides, you look really hot with a gag in your mouth."

Tanvi did as he asked, leaning back on her elbows and eyeing Alex warily as he walked around to the opposite side of the desk.

He grasped the end of her braid and tugged the band off, releasing her hair and running his hands through the thick strands. She tipped her head back and moaned around the handkerchief as Alex massaged her scalp. He dropped his head to hers. "I love your hair. Don't ever cut it."

He continued kneading her head, the sensations relaxing and soothing her until she forgot where they were.

Alex released her and walked around the desk so he was standing in front of her once more. He assessed her, his gaze traveling from her legs, to her torso and lingering on her breasts, his ice-blue eyes flashing hungrily. He lifted her skirt to her waist, revealing her plain cotton panties, and she wished fervently that she'd had the forethought to wear something even a little bit sexy.

"I love these." Alex urged a finger under the elastic waistband and caressed her mound. "They're sweet. Like you."

He tucked his thumbs in either side of her panties and started to sweep them down. She raised her hips off the desk to help him. He tossed them to the side and gazed at the juncture of her thighs. She was fast becoming used to his fondness for staring at her sex and she let him look his fill. He grasped her ankles and lifted her legs to place her feet flat on the desk, opening her wider to his perusal. She felt the moisture gathering, the blatant lust in his eyes driving her own.

"You're so wet, sweetness." He swiped a finger up her center then ran it around the lips of her pussy. "This is mine," he murmured, gazing at her and caressing her sex gently. "No one else touches this but me."

What does he mean? Tanvi had never seen this side of him. His eyes glinted possessively as he stroked her over and over, running her moisture through her cleft and around her outer lips, working her into a writhing mass of hormones.

Tanvi held her breath and bit down on her gag, trying to absorb the sensations like he'd taught her.

Alex grasped her hips and pulled her to the edge of the desk. "Grip the sides and don't let go."

He knelt in front of her, dipped his head between her thighs and inhaled. "Mmm, I can smell your arousal. It's. So. Fucking. Hot!"

He thrust two fingers into her and pushed them high and deep, locking his lips over her clit and sucking. A lightning bolt of sensation shot to her core and she arched off the desk. Pleasure coiled deep inside, firing her inner muscles into a quiver. He pumped his fingers and nipped her clit, and that was all it took. She came hard, the orgasm ripping through her body in a toe-curling, thigh-trembling release.

Alex lapped at her pussy, bringing her down gently from her climax. It was sexy and erotic watching his head bobbing between her legs. He raised his face, his chin glossy with her juices and licked his lips. "You taste so good, baby."

A shiver swept through her at his sensual words.

He stood swiftly and unbuttoned his shirt, shrugging it off his shoulders and tossing it aside. His chest was hard and sculpted and every time she looked at him, she couldn't quite believe that he was real. He undid his trousers but left them on, pushing his boxer briefs down to reveal his cock. He fished a condom out of his pocket, ripped the packet open and rolled the latex down his impressive erection.

"This is going to be hard and fast, sweetness. Grip the edge of the desk and don't let go." He grasped her knees, lined himself up and thrust deeply.

Tanvi groaned as Alex pushed his thick cock into her channel, stretching her impossibly wide.

"You are so hot and tight," he ground out between clenched teeth. "You feel so fucking good." He swept his hands down her thighs to grasp her hips and yank her forward as he pumped into her.

She kept a tight hold on the desk, the only thing keeping her from flying off the edge as Alex rammed into her. He grunted on each thrust, pushing so deep she could have sworn he bumped her cervix on each drive. She arched her hips up, changing the angle and sending him impossibly deeper.

Her insides trembled and tightened and pleasure ignited low in her belly.

"That's it," Alex yelled on a particularly hard thrust.

Tanvi held her breath and focused on the sensations erupting within her. She groaned low in her throat, her climax taking hold suddenly and intensely. She shuddered as her core contracted, milking Alex's cock and spurring him into orgasm. He thrust twice more, grinding his pelvis into hers and roaring her name.

Alex slumped on top of her for a moment, taking his weight with his arms while he worked to regulate his breathing. Finally, he lifted himself and removed the handkerchief from her mouth. He grabbed a handful of tissues and used them to gently clean between her legs.

She sat up and fixed her clothing.

"Pack an overnight bag," Alex instructed. "Tomorrow we're taking a trip. We leave in the afternoon, when you finish work."

What? "I can't just up and leave. I have responsibilities here."

"I'll talk to George. It'll be fine. Meet me in the lobby at four-thirty p.m."

Alex looked at his watch. "I have to go." He dropped a kiss to the top of her head. "Until tomorrow."

Chapter Nineteen

Tanvi packed up her desk and logged off her computer. She'd worked feverishly all day to clear as much as she could. She had no idea where Alex was taking her. However, she presumed it wasn't too far away. She'd asked him but he'd refused to tell her, stating that it was a surprise.

She found him waiting for her in the lobby, a small travel bag at his feet. He looked casual and handsome in cargo shorts that hugged his backside and a white open-necked linen shirt, sleeves rolled up to the elbows. He stepped forward and gave her a chaste kiss on the cheek.

"I've spoken to George and you're set to take tomorrow off. Sanjay is waiting for us out the front."

"Can you tell me where we are going now?"

He grasped her elbow and steered her toward the entrance. "We're going to the train station. Have you heard about the luxury train carriages that the Totally Five Star lease for the use of their guests?"

She had heard of the service. For an additional cost, hotel customers could use the carriages exclusively. "Yes, I've often wondered what they are like."

"You're about to find out. I've booked us a cabin. We're going to Agra."

"We're visiting the Taj Mahal?" She clapped with excitement. "I saw it when I was a young girl on a school trip and I've always wanted to go back."

Alex gave her a warm smile. "I'm glad you're excited. I've wanted to see it for a long time and we'll be traveling in style."

Sanjay was waiting by the SUV, back doors open in readiness. He bounced on the balls of his feet when he spotted them emerging through the hotel doors. "Boss, Ms. Sharma!" he called to them enthusiastically.

Tanvi grinned widely at him. She liked Alex's driver, he was friendly and courteous and always seemed to be in high spirits. Alex assisted her into the car then climbed in beside her as Sanjay placed their bags in the back.

* * * *

Tanvi hadn't caught a train in a long while and she'd forgotten how busy the station could be. It was a bustling mass of humanity. People scurried around with bags, suitcases and all manner of odd belongings. There was barely any space to walk and the sheer number of people had her feeling a little intimidated. Obviously she'd spent too much time lately in the cool, refined interior of the Totally Five Star. She was forgetting what the rest of India was like!

A train with numerous carriages was sitting at the platform. Alex grasped Tanvi's hand tightly as they followed Sanjay, their bags perched on the driver's head as he made a path through the throng of people. Finally, the last two carriages of the snaking train came into view. They were brightly painted, striped in red and green, with the Totally Five Star emblem on each side.

A conductor was waiting by the doors of the first carriage. "Mr. Banks?" he asked when they reached him.

Alex nodded and passed the man some paperwork.

"Welcome. I'll be your conductor and will assist in anything you need. Please come aboard."

Sanjay handed their bags to the conductor, and Tanvi and Alex followed the man onto the luxury car. Tanvi stared around in awe. It was like something out of a movie she'd once seen. The walls were paneled in a light grain wood, little shade lamps provided subtle lighting at intervals along the passageway and red carpet lined the floor.

The conductor ushered them into the first suite. A double, four-poster bed sat against the opposite wall, a sumptuous bedspread in green and gold covered the mattress and fat matching cushions had been tossed on top. There was a small sitting area at the front of the bed upholstered in striped green and gold satin and a two-seat round dining table under the window to the left. A door set into the left wall of the cabin, she guessed, was the bathroom, and next to that was an ornate wooden closet for clothes. On the right wall, opposite the closet, was a matching wooden sideboard with miniature bottles of liquor and crystal glasses on top.

Tanvi vaguely registered the conductor explaining details of the cabin to Alex as she absorbed the luxurious surroundings. She couldn't quite believe she would be staying in such a beautiful suite on a train — it was almost surreal. She felt as if she were in a mini palace.

"Dinner will be served at seven-thirty p.m. You will find the menu on the dining table and I'll call for your order at six," the conductor finished explaining. "I'll leave you alone now. Please press this call button if you need anything."

The conductor closed the door quietly behind him and Tanvi squealed, spinning around in a circle before collapsing on a sofa.

Alex chuckled. "It's beautiful, isn't it?"

"It's divine," Tanvi declared. "I can barely believe we're here. I had no idea it was so luxurious. How many cabins are there?"

"Four in each carriage. The main food is prepared in a separate dining car but there is a small butler's pantry in these carriages to reheat and prepare small meals."

Tanvi jumped up. "I haven't seen the bathroom." She walked over to the door stenciled with WC and opened it. Inside there was a toilet, a large basin, plush emerald-green towels and a round tub-shower recess with a white shower curtain tied to one side with a gold braid. In the corner sat a small-mirrored vanity, a little satin-upholstered stool in front. "It's charming," she proclaimed enthusiastically. "I love it!"

Tanvi's joy and enthusiasm were infectious and Alex was glad that he'd splurged on the luxurious travel option. He'd wanted to visit the Taj Mahal for a long time, but hadn't relished the thought of seeing such a beautiful and romantic place alone. This trip had seemed like the perfect excuse to travel to the famous World Heritage Site and also spend some time alone with Tanvi. They would be traveling via Jaipur, which meant the journey would take longer than usual.

He took Tanvi's hand and drew her toward the sitting area. "I take it you're familiar with the history of the Taj Mahal," he said.

"Of course. It's sad but very romantic. The Mughal emperor Shah Jahan had the temple built for his third and favorite wife, upon whom he had bestowed the title of Mumtaz Mahal, which means Chosen One of the Palace. They were engaged when he was fifteen and she was fourteen but were married five years later, when the court astrologers decided the date was the most auspicious. By all reports, they were inseparable. She was by far his favorite wife, his others, apparently, only having the status of marriage but never sharing the deep affection that Shah Jahan and Mumtaz Mahal shared." Tanvi sighed. "She died giving birth to their thirteenth child and Shah Jahan built the Taj Mahal in her memory and to house her tomb. He was inconsolable about her death and apparently went into secluded mourning for a year. Then, when he finally emerged, he'd aged considerably. She truly was the love of his life."

"A very romantic history to the Taj Mahal," Alex agreed. "It will be a joy to see it with you by my side."

Tanvi smiled and her cheeks pinked at his assertion. Alex looked at his watch. "We need to look at the menu and decide what we want for dinner." He placed the menu in front of them. "How about we share the *biryani* with no nuts and a salad?"

"That sounds delicious. Do I have time for a shower? I'd like to freshen up before dinner."

"Of course. I had one before we left the hotel. There's an array of products in the cupboard in the bathroom."

A sharp whistle sounded outside and the train shuddered to life. "It looks like we'll be leaving in a minute. Be careful in the bathroom," Alex instructed as Tanvi gathered her toiletries.

"I will," she assured him, blowing him a kiss before slipping through the WC door.

Chapter Twenty

Tanvi luxuriated in the shower. There were a number of shower jets fitted to give the bather an extra special treat. She tried them all, adjusting the pressure and direction of the jets to get a body massage. She lathered all over with the jasmine-scented body wash and shampooed and conditioned her hair with the special products provided by the hotel. The train lurched into motion and she grasped the safety handle to steady herself. Her heart gave an excited thud. There was something thrilling about taking such a luxurious shower on a train while in motion.

Alex opened the door and stuck his head in. "Are you okay?"

Tanvi ducked her head out of the snowy-white shower curtain. "I'm fine," she called gaily. "I'm just experimenting with all the knobs and buttons in here."

Alex laughed. "If you stay in there any longer, you'll turn into a prune. Just remember that we're moving. I don't want you to hurt yourself."

She ducked her head back in to rinse off the conditioner. "I will. I'll be out in a minute." Alex's concern for her well-being was gratifying. She frowned, wondering why such a simple act of caring should be so pleasing to her. She felt different, though, more alive since she'd met Alex, and she had to admit that his thoughtfulness was definitely part of his charm. She was determined to make the most of their time together — her initial reticence had long since vanished. She was now firmly in Tanvi and Alex territory. All her misgivings about Rakesh and her uncle, she'd pushed to the back of her mind, compartmentalizing them to a dark corner. It was only Alex she was focused on.

She turned the water off and grabbed one of the fluffy emerald-green towels. Her hair would take an age to dry, but she couldn't resist using the lovely scented products and, as they wouldn't be leaving the cabin, it didn't matter if her hair remained damp.

She rummaged in her bag for the satin nightdress with the matching gown that she'd packed. It was a royal blue with spaghetti straps and a deep lace-edged neckline. She slipped it on, relishing the feel of the fabric sliding against her shower-sensitive skin. She spritzed herself lightly with perfume and applied a coconut oil conditioner to the ends of her hair. She'd brush it out a little later.

When Tanvi stepped back into the suite, Alex was reclining on one of the sofas, reading a book about Agra and the Taj Mahal that had been sitting on the coffee table. A bottle of white wine was chilling in a silver ice bucket. He looked up, his gaze traveling over her body appreciatively, and she couldn't miss the lust clouding his eyes.

Jasmine Hill

"You're gorgeous," he murmured. "I love that color on you."

"Thank you." She didn't think she'd ever get tired of his compliments. She motioned to the book in his hands. "You're reading up on the history."

"Yes. It's interesting and I want to know what I'm looking at tomorrow."

Alex poured them each a glass of wine then placed a fat cushion on the floor between his feet and motioned to her. "Come sit in front of me. I want to brush your hair."

She'd completely forgotten about the brush in her hand. She handed it to Alex and accepted a glass of wine in return then settled herself on the cushion. She took a sip from her glass, relishing the crisp, light fruitiness. She'd never been a big fan before, but this wine was delicious. "Where is the wine from?"

Alex took a sip of his own then placed his glass on the coffee table. "From Australia, the Margret River region. They do a fabulous Sauvignon Blanc. The Totally Five Star has an extensive cellar. I ordered it when I booked the cabin."

He dropped his mouth to her ear and inhaled deeply. "You smell so good, like jasmine and coconut, exotic and delicious."

Her insides quivered with anticipation. No man had ever been able to wring such sensuous responses out of her so quickly, but all it took from Alex was a couple of sexy words spoken in that low, hot accent of his.

Alex took hold of her thick rope of hair and draped it over his lap. "Put your head back," he ordered.

She did as he instructed and felt the strong bristles of the brush as he started at her hairline and stroked through to the ends. She moaned in appreciation — the sensation of the stiff bristles on her scalp divine.

It was odd, Alex had never before felt the need to brush a woman's hair, but with Tanvi, he was different. He loved the feel of her lustrous tresses as they sifted through his fingers. He swept the brush through the thick strands over and over again until her hair shone and the scent of coconut wafted around them in an enticing aroma. His cock swelled hard and insistent against the zipper of his shorts and he shifted on the sofa to alleviate his discomfort. He looked at his watch — six-forty. They had fifty minutes until dinner would arrive — plenty of time for a quick romp.

"I think you're done," he said quietly, placing the brush on the sofa next to him. "Now I need to relieve an irritating ache that's set in."

Tanvi looked up at him, inhaling sharply. He smiled at her response — so eager, but nervous with it. She slid her hand up his calf, along his thigh then cupped his throbbing erection. He groaned and lifted his hips, forcing his cock harder into her palm. "That feels good, baby, but now I want you on the bed and on your back. Eyes closed."

She rose gracefully to her feet and scurried to do his bidding. He loved that she did whatever he instructed, no questions asked. He selected the Evanescence *Fallen* album on the iPod docking station then strode to the long, rectangular window and lowered the shade. He stared down at the bed. Tanvi was lying as instructed with her eyes closed. Her ebony hair fanned out over the pillows like a silken veil. Her chest was heaving, little inhalations that plumped her breasts and told him that her heart rate had sped up. *Is she nervous or excited?*

He caressed her cheek with his finger and she jumped a little at the contact.

"Are you anxious, sweetness?"

"No," she breathed. "I trust you."

Fuck, she was perfect for him. "Good," he murmured. "You don't have anything to fear from me." He opened a bedside drawer and withdrew a number of sex toys and two pairs of fur-lined handcuffs that he'd put there when Tanvi was showering. "I'm going to bind your wrists to the bedposts. I have one set of handcuffs for each post."

She nodded and dropped her head to the side, eyes still closed. She looked serene and relaxed, exactly how he wanted her.

He swiftly attached the cuffs to each post, lengthened the chains to accommodate the width of the bed then snapped her wrists into the bindings. "The key to open these is right here on the bedside table," he murmured. "I won't ever leave you while you're bound. Do you understand?"

"Yes."

He frowned. It was time that he taught her about discipline and the use of his preferred title when he engaged in this type of play.

"Yes, what, Tanvi?"

Confusion clouded her features. "I don't understand."

"You will address me as sir or Mr. Banks."

Her eyes grew wide. "Are you serious?"

"Very," he stated in his Dom voice. "Let's try that again. Do you understand that I won't leave you alone and you know where the key is?"

"Yes, sir."

"Good girl." Alex tested the cuffs to ensure that they weren't too tight.

The music morphed to Evanescence's *Haunted*, perfect for what he intended. He tied a scarf around Tanvi's head, blindfolding her. "I'm going to limit your senses again. Only focus on the music and what I'm doing to you."

"Yes, sir," she murmured complacently.

He rummaged in the drawer again and found the pair of vibrating nipple clamps. He adjusted them to a resistance he felt that Tanvi could handle. Grasping the neckline of her gown, he then pulled it down until her breasts were pushed up and over the fabric. He dipped his head and sucked one nipple deep into his mouth, drawing on the stiffened peak until it puckered and elongated, flicking the tip with his tongue. He applied the same technique to her other nipple and attached both clamps, switching them on to a mild vibration.

Tanvi gasped, her mouth wide and slack as the sensations took hold. Alex studied her for a moment, letting her adjust to the pressure of the clamps. When he was satisfied that she was comfortable, he switched the vibrations to the next level.

She groaned and bowed off the bed, the motion pushing her chest up and emphasizing her breasts jiggling with the slight vibrations. He growled low in his throat, his cock rock-hard and throbbing insistently. She looked so fucking hot right now, bound and at his mercy. The silken blue of her gown shimmered over her body as she writhed, almost like it had a life of its own, slipping and sliding over her taut tummy and lush hips.

Alex stepped closer to the bed and grasped the shiny fabric of her gown, sweeping it up over her pelvis to reveal the neat thatch of pubic hair between her thighs. He gripped each of her ankles and spread them wide.

Immediately, her lush scent hit him, her spicy arousal mingling with the scent of jasmine and coconut to drive him wild. He stopped for a moment, closed his eyes and breathed deeply, reining in the feral lust coursing through his veins.

"Keep your legs spread like this," he ordered, his voice tight with need. "Don't move."

She whimpered and bowed off the bed once more, but kept her thighs positioned where he'd placed them.

Alex stepped back from the bed and undressed quickly, his gaze trained all the while on Tanvi as she mewed softly. Her pubic hair was glistening invitingly, her juices trickling between her thighs.

His cock and balls were aching desperately now. As he was denying her, he was denying himself. He prided himself on his control and his willpower, but this woman was stripping him of that, like no other ever had.

He walked to the bedside table, his erection standing thick and rigid against his abdomen and bouncing painfully as he moved. He adjusted Tanvi's nipple clamps to the highest setting and she groaned, a low guttural sound that told him she was nearing her endurance.

"Are you okay, baby?" he asked. "Remember your safe word?"

"Yes, sir," she panted. "I'm good."

He was impressed with her stamina and decided not to prolong her agony any longer. He picked up a clit stimulator from the bedside table and positioned himself back between her legs. He attached the vibe to her clit and turned it on to a medium setting. Immediately, she whimpered, her mouth forming a perfect 'O' as the stimulus attacked her sensitive nerves.

Alex flicked the setting to a touch higher and she arched her back, her legs stiffening. She cried out, a garbled, broken sound. He pushed two fingers into her warm, wet heat and felt the pulses of her inner muscles as they contracted around him.

"I can feel it when you come," he said thickly. "It's exquisite."

He switched the vibe off for a moment to give her time to recover. This wasn't about enforced orgasms. He was testing her limits and her ability to control her pleasure. Her thighs were trembling slightly as she worked through the vestiges of her climax. He narrowed his gaze on her heaving chest. Her nipples were erect and extended under the clamps, her breasts jiggling with the vibrations.

He groaned and swept two fingers around her juicy cleft. She gasped and bucked under his touch. *Fuck, I can't take any more!*

He switched the clit stimulator back on and increased the vibrations to high.

"Argh," she cried out, gripping the cuff chains until her knuckles turned white.

Alex climbed onto the bed and straddled her torso. "I'm going to fuck these beautiful breasts," he murmured, grasping his cock and pumping his fist along his length. Pre-cum gathered on his tip, oozing out in thick white beads. He spread his moisture in Tanvi's cleavage, flattening his palm between her plump mounds and reaching behind him to sweep his fingers through her slick heat. He used her juices to lubricate his cock and reached forward to remove her blindfold. He wanted her to watch this.

Her gaze zeroed in on his bobbing erection and her breathing accelerated. She licked her lips, made plump and red from where she'd been biting them.

"You have me all over you," he grated as he squeezed more pre-cum from his tip and spread it around the swells of her cleavage. "And I have you all over me."

He cupped each of her breasts, palming the outsides and pushing them together. He thrust his cock between the fleshy globes and groaned, a guttural, primal sound that emanated from deep in his belly. "Fuck!"

He started a slow, sensual glide, the vibrations of the nipple clamps traveling through Tanvi's breasts and into his cock, tightening his balls. Lust clawed at the base of his spine and heat coiled in his abdomen.

He locked his gaze on her face and knew the exact instant she came again. Her eyes widened and she stiffened beneath him, shouting his name.

"That's it, baby. Work through it. You'll come again in a minute, that vibe is working you right where you're most sensitive."

She gazed at him under heavy lids, her jaw slack, perspiration dotting her forehead. She looked close to passing out and he hadn't even actually fucked her.

He quickened his thrusts, squeezing her breasts around his dick to heighten the vibrations. Pleasure boiled and settled deep in his gut and his balls drew up close to his body.

Tanvi opened her mouth, her eyes imploring him. He thrust harder until she caught his cock in her mouth and sucked on the bulbous head, his apadravya hitting her teeth at each entry.

"I'm going to come," he grated. He could feel her body trembling beneath him and knew she was close. "I want you to come again."

She could only nod, her mouth so full of his swollen cock that one cheek bulged. The sight of her, so complete with him, sent him over the edge. His balls constricted and cum bubbled along his length. He wanted to come on her — to mark her. He pulled out of her mouth and pumped between her breasts like an animal. Pleasure scorched through him and he grunted low in his throat as he spurted his seed over her face spectacularly. His orgasm was so intense it left him momentarily blinded. He vaguely registered Tanvi bucking beneath him and crying out in her own release.

Chapter Twenty-One

Alex's blurred vision recovered and he quickly removed the vibe from Tanvi's clit. Her damp hair lay plastered to her forehead, the nipple clamps still buzzing away. He released one clamp and quickly replaced it with his mouth, sucking and soothing her tortured nipple. He did the same with the other, ensuring that the rush of blood to the sensitive tip was eased.

He drew back and gazed at her face, so lovely and relaxed in post-orgasmic bliss, her eyelids so heavy that he couldn't see the wonderful green of her eyes.

"Are you okay, sweetness?" He brushed a soft kiss over her lips. "Are you tired?"

"Hmm," she mumbled sleepily.

Alex jumped off the bed and strode into the bathroom to wet a washcloth. Tanvi smelled like him and he was loath to wash it off but he didn't think she'd appreciate eating dinner with his cum all over her. He swiped the cloth gently over her face and neck then down across her clavicle and breasts. His gaze alighted on her nipples, still elongated from the clamps.

He dropped his mouth to one and sucked on it gently, then he licked a trail to the other and sucked there. He drew his head back and blew softly over her damp flesh. She squirmed, arched her back and moaned.

"Are they sore, baby?"

She yawned and stretched her arms above her head, the action plumping her breasts deliciously.

"Yes, but I'd do it all over again." She gave him a saucy look. "I can feel the vibrations all the way to here." She swept her hand down her torso and trailed her fingers through her still-damp pussy.

Alex growled, his eyes riveted on her hand between her thighs. His cock stood to attention, thick and hard and already brushing his belly button. Christ, he was insatiable when it came to her.

"Don't tempt me, princess. Any moment now our dinner will be delivered and we need to freshen up."

* * * *

Dinner was delicious, a moist and spicy chicken biryani and a crisp salad, which they washed down with the remainder of the wine.

Tanvi stretched and yawned—her three orgasms before dinner, combined with the hypnotic movement of the train, were making her sleepy. The bed was looking extremely inviting and she was having trouble keeping her eyes open. Before she could say anything, Alex leaned across the small dining room table and took her hand in his.

"You look worn out," he murmured. "Why don't we get ready for bed? It's an early start tomorrow and remember we stop at one of the stations for a couple of hours so don't get startled when the train stops for any length of time."

She smiled her appreciation, always just a little surprised at his consideration.

Alex stood, the impressive bulge in his boxers sending a tingle through her. He'd eaten dressed only in his briefs and his sculpted chest had diverted her attention more than once over dinner.

He started clearing the dishes. "I'll place these outside the door as the waiter instructed. You go on in and use the bathroom."

Tanvi scurried into the en suite, scrubbed her face, moisturized and brushed her teeth. She peered at her reflection in the vanity mirror. Her green eyes sparkled and her cheeks were flushed. Even she could see the difference in her appearance since she'd met Alex. The changes were subtle, but anyone who knew her well would surely see a transformation. Her usual, serious and sometimes tight expression had been replaced with something almost carefree. The reasons behind her solemnity still existed, however, and, for the second time that evening, she shoved the thought to the far recesses of her mind. She ran her fingers through her hair in attempt to tame the wild mane. All that romping around on the bed with damp hair had left her with a serious case of bed head. She drew back from the mirror and gave her reflection another critical assessment. *Yes, I like this look.* Her ebony tresses cascaded down her back and around her shoulders in a wavy, tousled mass. *I look sassy...sexy,* she decided. Perhaps she'd do as Alex had asked—no, ordered—and not cut her hair after all.

She jumped when Alex stuck his head through the door, smiling to herself at his lack of discretion. She guessed he wouldn't have cared less if she'd been on the toilet and perhaps would have even gotten a kick out of it, the kinky bastard.

"I'm finished," she announced. "Your turn."

She slipped past him and started to tidy the suite, picking up Alex's shirt and shorts and draping them over the back of a chair.

She smiled as she recalled Alex's absurd behavior when their meal had arrived. The young waiter had knocked on the door with their dinner tray, and Alex, rather than allowing him entrance, had whisked the tray out of the startled man's hands and brought the meal in himself. At Tanvi's questioning look, he'd explained that he didn't want anyone seeing her wearing such an alluring outfit. She'd been a little baffled — having donned her matching gown she'd thought she looked quite presentable, but apparently Alex hadn't agreed.

Turning around, she spied her overnight bag and remembered the outfit she'd packed to wear the following day. The *shalwar kameez* was by a new designer, experimenting with a fusion of traditional Indian with some Western influence. She loved it, but the fabric crushed easily and she needed to hang it. She removed the garments from her small suitcase and shook out the creases as she walked over to the ornate closet. She opened the door and stopped dead in her tracks, terror rooting her to the spot before a blood-curdling scream erupted involuntarily from her throat.

Chapter Twenty-Two

Alex had just finished washing up when Tanvi's scream ripped through the air, a sound so chilling that the hairs on the back of his neck stood up. His blood turned to ice. *Tanvi!* Fear for her safety galvanized him into immediate action.

He shot out of the bathroom door and landed in the suite, his body tensed for violence. He grabbed the first makeshift weapon he could lay his hands on, an umbrella from the rack to the right of the closet. Tanvi was in front of the open closet doors, her body trembling as she stared, wide-eyed, at something he couldn't see.

He stepped to the left, instinctively keeping his movements slow and steady. He needed to see what had Tanvi so transfixed with terror. As the interior of the closet came into view, the air left his lungs. On the floor in front of the open doors lay a snake, coiled, head up ready to strike. Alex didn't know much about snakes in India, but he did know that next to Australia, the country had some of the deadliest in the world. It was clear that when Tanvi had opened the doors, she'd disturbed it and there weren't too many things more dangerous than an angry serpent.

"Tanvi, stay very still, baby. Don't move." He kept his tone low and soothing.

"Alex?" Her voice was barely a whisper and tinged with anxiety.

"I'm here, sweetness. Just focus on not moving."

His brain raced as he thought wildly about what to do. He assessed the snake and guessed it was about five feet in length. It had a flattish head and black body banded with white stripes. *What the fuck is it?* He didn't know if it was lethal but he wasn't about to take any chances. He looked at the umbrella in his hand. It was sturdy and heavy, the type you use when playing golf. In his other hand, he still held the towel he was using when Tanvi had screamed.

He crept closer, keeping his eyes trained on the snake. The thing was focused on Tanvi as its immediate threat, allowing Alex to move closer.

"I'm right here, baby," he assured her quietly. "You're doing fine. You're keeping really still. That's good."

The only thing he could do was to kill it. He didn't have the equipment, or the know-how to remove it safely. He hoped it wasn't some rare, endangered species, or something revered under Indian mythology. But his options were limited and God knew how far away they were from any medical facilities.

Alex breathed deeply and gathered his wits about him. There was no room for error, no room for second-guessing himself or fucking up. He took one slow step forward to bring himself level with Tanvi. At the movement so close to her, the snake switched its focus to Alex. It hissed, its long forked tongue flicking out with the sound. Alex wasted no time. He threw the towel over the snake's head to disorient it and, brandishing the umbrella in two hands, he whacked it down, hard. The elongated body writhed and slithered, its tail thrashing as Alex brought the umbrella down again, snapping the snake's spine and killing it in two strikes.

Sweat had broken out on his brow and he was breathing heavily, the adrenaline spiking through him, leaving him shaky and off kilter.

Tanvi let out a little cry then launched herself into his arms, trembling uncontrollably.

"Shh," he hushed her, rubbing her back in big circles. "It's the fear and the adrenaline, baby. Breathe through it."

He held her tightly, soothing her with low, murmured words and rhythmic strokes to her spine until she started to settle. He glanced around the suite and caught site of the minibar.

Alex released Tanvi, strode to the sideboard and poured a little bottle of scotch into a glass. He returned to her and urged her to sit, pressing the glass into her hand. "Drink this," he ordered. "It will settle your nerves."

She brought the glass up to her lips, the crystal rattling against her teeth as she took a deep drink.

Alex shoved a hand through his hair and glared at the dead snake. *How the hell did the thing end up in the suite, and in the closet no less?* He needed to get rid of it and speak to the conductor. He grabbed the fabric wash bag from one of the shelves, picked the snake up by the tail and shoved it into the bag. He rummaged through his luggage for a pair of sweatpants and pulled them on.

He squatted in front of Tanvi's chair. "I'm going to find the conductor. Will you be okay here alone for a few minutes?" He stroked her cheek with his thumb.

She nodded and he was relieved to see some color returning to her features. He bent forward and placed a soft kiss on her lips. "I won't be long."

Alex stalked down the passageway toward a cabin that he'd seen the conductor disappear into. He rapped loudly and heard movement on the other side. The door opened and the conductor greeted him. "Can I help you, sir?"

"You most certainly can," Alex snarled. "We had an unwanted visitor."

The conductor looked on in confusion as Alex opened the cloth bag and emptied the contents at his feet. The man cried out and stumbled back a few steps.

"It's okay," Alex said dryly. "It's dead. I killed it. Do you know what it is?"

The conductor recovered himself and stepped forward to tentatively examine the snake. He looked up at Alex, eyes wide. "It's an Indian krait," he whispered, his face pale.

"Is it dangerous?"

"Yes, it kills many people in India."

"How the fuck did it get into our suite?" Alex demanded angrily. "It could have killed my girlfriend. She disturbed it when she opened the closet doors." Abstractedly, he registered his use of the unfamiliar girlfriend title. He'd have to examine that later.

"I-I don't know, sir," the conductor stammered, clearly mortified. "I will lodge a report with my superiors. I don't know how it gained entry to the suite. It is very strange, sir."

It *was* strange all right. Alex found it hard to believe the snake just slithered in of its own accord. The whole incident left a cold feeling of apprehension in his gut. If the snake in their suite was not, in fact, an accident, then who the fuck had planted it there and why?

* * * *

Tanvi finished the scotch, welcoming the warmth that it spread to her shivering limbs. She rose to her feet a little unsteadily and walked to the bed. Suddenly the weariness that had threatened to overwhelm her earlier was back with a vengeance and she could hardly keep her eyes open. She pulled the covers down and slipped between the cool sheets. Vaguely she heard the suite door opening, then Alex was looming over her. He squatted by her side, rested his palm on her temple and brushed back her hair.

"How are you feeling?"

"Better, thank you." She wanted him next to her, needed to feel his strong, warm body against hers. As if he read her mind, he stood swiftly and undressed, then he climbed into bed and pulled her body tightly to his. He spooned her, the thick flesh between his legs resting in the crevice of her ass, his broad palm cupping one of her breasts. She snuggled into him, relishing the feel of his hard chest against her back, his powerful proximity soothing her.

"Sleep now," he whispered into her ear. "You're safe."

And she knew she was.

Chapter Twenty-Three

After a full night's sleep and a delicious breakfast, Tanvi felt in much higher spirits. If she hadn't known better, she could almost have believed that the events of the previous evening were some kind of dream. They'd been lucky — extremely lucky. Alex had told her that morning that the snake was an Indian krait. She didn't want to dwell on how or why it had ended up in their suite. She was just beyond thankful that Alex had been there, and that his quick thinking and bold actions had saved her from a possibly fatal bite.

"We're here," Alex announced as their car pulled to a stop outside of the Taj Mahal main entrance and ticket area.

She'd been so wrapped up in her thoughts that she hadn't even noticed where they were. They purchased their tickets and made their way toward the mausoleum. Numerous guides, ID cards hanging around their necks, clamored to get their attention. She stopped and spoke to one and quickly negotiated a price for a guided tour. She hadn't visited the Taj Mahal since she was a young girl and she found that she wanted the information that the guide would be able to give them. It was also important that Alex get the most out of the experience.

They walked through the grand red-brick arch of the Darwaza gateway to the Taj Mahal and immediately met the watercourse, a beautiful sparkling path leading to the mausoleum. The image was stunning and beautifully picturesque. Alex grasped Tanvi's hand and they stopped for a moment to admire the view. The famous tomb was absolutely majestic, the marble shining white and gleaming in the sunlight. They walked slowly along, their guide pointing out architectural details and discussing the history. Lotus-shaped fountains adorned the four ponds. They passed the stone bench where the infamous photo of Princess Diana had been taken and reached the grand reflecting pool where each of the four pools converged, the reflection of the Taj Mahal glittering on the surface in a shimmery echo.

Tanvi was mesmerized. It was so much grander and more beautiful than she remembered. Even the gardens, or Charbagh, as the guide explained, were spectacular. Laid out in the traditional Mughal quadrilateral design and divided by the four pools of the watercourse.

It was symbolic and tranquil and one of the most beautiful places she'd ever seen. She definitely hadn't appreciated it as a young girl. Visiting it now, with Alex by her side, seemed almost a pilgrimage to romance. It would be obvious to all who looked upon the mausoleum that it was the ultimate monument to a deep love.

They reached the platform on which sat the Taj Mahal itself, their guide handing them white paper booties to place over their shoes in order to protect the sacred surfaces. Tanvi stared up at the walls of the structure, marveling at the Koranic script and elaborate floral designs reminiscent of the Mughal Empire that had been carved into the marble by thousands of expert craftsmen.

Their guide described the specialist work of the skilled artisans, the trade having been passed down through the generations. He explained how the thousands of men working on the massive mausoleum carved out the floral designs in the marble then inlaid the etchings with semi-precious stones using the *pietra dura* technique. Brandishing a penlight, the guide illuminated the colorful inlay to demonstrate a stained-glass-like effect.

He explained that it took approximately twenty-two years and roughly twenty thousand men to build the Taj Mahal. Tanvi was astounded. The mausoleum, in all its complex parts and flawless design, was a testament to the years of toil by artisans, architects and laborers and to Shah Jahan's undying love for his cherished wife. It was romantic, sad, beautiful and serene in equal measures.

"It's absolutely exquisite," Tanvi breathed in awe. "So much work by so many people."

They wandered around the structure, inspecting the minarets located on each of the four corners of the platform. They stopped and stared out across the Yamuna River at the Red Fort of Agra, and Alex wrapped an arm around her waist. Tanvi leaned into him, happy with their anonymity amid the many tourists. Their guide pointed across the river to the rooms where Shah Jahan spent the final years of his life. Having been imprisoned by his son in the Red Fort of Agra, he at least had the solace of being able to look upon the monument he'd so lovingly constructed for his wife.

Alex looked down at Tanvi. Her eyes shone and her cheeks glowed pink. It was obvious that she was enjoying herself and he thought the fresh air and gardens around the Taj Mahal were having an enlivening effect on her. He guessed that the time away from her family and New Delhi was also conducive to her relaxed mood. She didn't talk about her home life much but Tanvi seemed to always carry a trace of unease and discontent, which he suspected was due to something personal.

"Are you ready to go?" he asked her.

She gazed up at him and smiled. "Thank you so much for bringing me here, Alex. I guess I could visit any time, but I just never got around to it and I also enjoyed seeing it with you." She gave a little shrug. "It's special when you have someone you care about by your side."

Alex brushed his thumb down her cheek. "I enjoyed seeing it with you too." He looked at his watch. "Unfortunately, it's time to go. We'll have dinner on the train."

She sighed, a sadness shadowing her eyes. "I don't want to go home."

He grasped her hand and started slowly walking toward the exit. "I know, baby, but I'll make it up to you when we get back."

He didn't know just what he was going to do to surpass this trip, but he'd think of something. He frowned as he recalled the previous evening and the deadly snake in the closet. The incident made him uneasy and, as much as he tried, he just couldn't totally believe it was an accident. He'd interrogated the staff and none of them had given him a reasonable explanation as to how the thing had found its way into the suite. The alternative, however, was that someone had deliberately planted it there—but who and why? Why would someone want to hurt him or Tanvi? He couldn't think of any reasons. He had no enemies and he couldn't imagine Tanvi had any, but he didn't want to scare her by asking. She seemed to have put the incident behind her, which was for the best. Perhaps he should do the same thing. Ruminating on it was only making him edgy and getting him nowhere. No, he'd put it down to an accident, an unfortunate twist of fate, and leave it at that. One thing was for damn sure, though—he'd be checking every single nook and cranny in their suite before he'd allow Tanvi to step foot into it.

Chapter Twenty-Four

They arrived back in New Delhi in the early hours of the following morning. Tanvi was staying with Alex rather than returning to her house, which she was relieved about. The longer she stayed away from her childhood home, the longer she could forget about what her future had in store for her. She'd told her parents that she was staying at the hotel while she worked through some paperwork.

She'd slept well on the train and when they stepped through Alex's suite door, she felt energized and wide awake.

Alex walked into the kitchenette and popped a capsule into the Nespresso machine. "Coffee?"

"Please." Tanvi hopped onto the counter and watched as Alex pottered around, locating mugs and milk and pouring orange juice.

The scent of coffee filled the air and made her mouth water. She'd only fairly recently started drinking it, having been raised pretty much on chai, and she'd found she enjoyed the roasted, slightly bitter flavor of coffee, a pleasant change from the milky sweetness of Indian tea.

Alex prepared their coffees and handed her a mug as he nudged her legs apart and stood between them. They drank in silence — a comfortable silence — not one of those awkward times when someone would invariably feel the need to fill the void with random babble. They were relaxed in each other's presence, like an old married couple, she thought inexplicably.

Alex finished his coffee and placed his mug on the counter next to her. "Care for a bath?" He took her empty mug from her and placed it next to his. "Go into the bedroom. I want you undressed with your hair down. Wait for me."

Tanvi's heart fluttered and delicious anticipation sluiced through her veins. She hurried to do his bidding, anxious to see what he'd do to her.

She walked into the bedroom, wriggled out of her jeans and unbuttoned her cotton blouse before shrugging it to the floor.

She gazed at her lingerie-clad body in the mirror. Her breasts swelled in anticipation, her desire making them fuller and rounder, her nipples already elongated, cherry red and pushing against the lace of her bra. Her gaze traveled lower, over her flat stomach, across her rounded hips and settled on the little triangle of cloth between her thighs. The satin was damp from her arousal, but she wasn't embarrassed as she would have been before she met Alex. She knew he'd find the evidence of her need for him to be a huge turn-on.

Patchouli-scented steam drifted from the bathroom, the exotic aroma arousing her further and sending her senses tingling. She closed her eyes and breathed deeply, inhaling the spicy scent and willing her body to relax. A slight shift in the air, a subtle awareness, had her eyes popping back open.

Alex stood behind her, a towel wrapped around his lean waist, his muscular chest bare and gleaming wetly from the steam of the bathroom. "I ordered you to undress." He clicked his tongue in annoyance. "And you know how I like your hair."

His voice was deep and husky and sent a shiver of longing rippling down her spine.

He grasped her braid, pulled the band off the end and unraveled the tresses. He gathered a thick strand in his fist and wrapped it around his wrist, tugging her head back. "But as it happens," he continued, his voice low and hypnotic against her ear, "I happen to like this lingerie. It highlights your arousal clearly and very sexily. I can see that you're wet for me and your breasts are swelling."

He released her hair and cupped her breasts in his palms, pinching her nipples and tugging gently.

Tanvi moaned and swayed against him, arching into his hands, needing more friction to that sensitive part of her.

"Your breasts are engorged with your desire, the blood vessels are dilating, expanding." His voice was whisper soft, and the sensation, combined with his rhythmic pulling, had her nipples elongating painfully. "Your cheeks and neck are flushed and your breathing is rapid."

He released her right breast and smoothed his palm down her side, over her hip to cup her sex through her panties. "And this, this will tell me exactly what's happening to your body."

Tanvi watched their reflection in the mirror under hooded lids, the visual so stimulating that she felt another rush of moisture between her thighs.

Alex cupped her sex, caressing her with the flat of his palm, his gaze meeting hers, his eyes knowing and bright with lust. "Here, you're wet, so wet for me, baby." He massaged her rhythmically with the flat of his palm. "I can feel how hard your little clit is. It's erect from the blood flow and your sweet pussy is swollen from your need."

He thrust his hips against her lower back, grinding his thick cock against her.

"I can smell you too." He slipped a finger under the elastic of her panties and brushed her clit lightly.

She startled and jumped. She was so sensitive there that she imagined even the gentlest touch would set her off.

"Oh fuck," he groaned as he slipped his finger inside her. "You're sopping and so fucking swollen."

Suddenly Alex pulled her off her feet, turned her body and, cupping her ass with one hand, he used the other to wrap her legs around his waist. "I need to take you quickly, I'm too far gone."

He strode over to a dresser with her wrapped easily around his waist, like she weighed no more than a bag of flour. There was the scrape of metal then a pair of scissors materialized in front of her face and she stiffened.

"Shh, baby. I'm not going to hurt you."

Alex placed the scissors against the flesh between her breasts. There was a snap then her bra popped open, cut in two. He did the same to her panties, snipping them on each side then flinging the shredded fabric aside.

"Tell me you're on the pill? I'm clean and I want in you bare if you'll allow."

Tanvi could hardly muster a coherent thought, so wild was she with need for him. "I-I'm on the pill," she confirmed, her voice trembling. "And I'm safe too. I have no disea—"

Her words were cut off abruptly as he thrust into her hard and to the hilt. She moaned as his thick erection pierced through her swollen tissues.

"Oh, Christ," he groaned as he stilled inside her. "You feel so fucking good, so wet and tight and silky."

He cupped her ass and bounced her on his cock, thrusting up hard with his hips.

She felt so full with him, so overwhelmed, she thought she could feel him brushing up against her womb. She whimpered and gripped his shoulders, her fingernails biting into his bulging muscles.

"That's it," he declared raggedly. "Hurt me."

She grasped him harder and he swung them around, her back hitting the wall with a thud. He reared back then plunged again, the force sending her skimming up the wall.

"You're. Not. Getting. Away," he declared on each thrust into her, gripping her ass and yanking her onto his cock.

Tanvi threw her head back and wrapped her legs tighter around his waist as he pumped into her like a man possessed, his balls slapping against her ass on each plunge.

"You have to come soon," he ground out. "I'm too fucking close."

His cock swelled and kicked inside her, spurring her core's fluttering and tightening.

"That's it," he urged, his voice hot against her ear. "You're nearly there."

She clenched her inner muscles, gripping him and holding tight.

"Sweet Jesus," he hissed and stilled inside her, breathing deeply. "You're gonna make me come too quickly. I need you to get there fast!"

Slowly, he withdrew then plunged up once more, seating his cock deeply.

She cried out as pleasure coalesced and swelled inside her, spurring a pulsing, throbbing in her sex.

Alex stared up into her eyes, his gaze holding her captive, his blue orbs blazing wild with lust and hunger. Sweat dotted his brow and the muscles of his neck bulged. He pulled back, dragging his shaft inexorably through the swollen folds of her pussy, the barbell on his cock hitting her sensitive clit and sending her spiraling into a mind-numbing, tumultuous orgasm.

Tanvi screamed his name as her vision flashed white and she bucked and trembled in his arms.

Alex growled, a feral sound emanating from deep in his throat. He thrust faster and pumped harder, gripping Tanvi's hips and grinding his pelvis into hers.

Tanvi's rhythmic milking of his cock, as she worked through her orgasm, sent him positively cross-eyed. His balls tightened and the base of his spine tensed. He widened his stance for better balance and used the wall to support Tanvi's body. He swept his hands up her torso and gripped her under the arms, anchoring her shoulders against the wall. He held her there and pumped his hips up, driving his throbbing cock as deeply as he could. Fuck, he was so deep he bumped against her cervix on each thrust. The erotic visual and the feel of her tight heat fisting him sent him over the edge and he came, hard. His abdominals tightened and he barked a curse as his cock jerked and his cum shot out of him and deep into her. He held Tanvi up and shuddered against her. His release emanated through him in a powerful undulating wave, blurring his vision and leaving him weak in the knees.

Alex rested a moment, supporting Tanvi between the wall and his body while he regained his vision and his breath. Slowly, he allowed her to slide down and onto her feet. He cupped her ass, yanked her to him and dropped his head to inhale her scent. She smelled of jasmine and sex and...him. It was so hot, almost like he'd branded her, claimed her as his, and he guessed he had when he thought about his cum deep inside her.

Suddenly the need to taste himself on her overwhelmed him and he dropped to his knees, urged her back against the wall and swept one of her legs over his shoulder.

She gasped as he shoved his head between her thighs and thrust his tongue deep inside her sex. She moaned and gripped his hair as he sucked and lapped at her. Fuck, she was hot and swollen and slick with his cum. He swept his tongue around her pussy lips and located her clit. The little bud was tight and still erect from her arousal and orgasm. He growled into her, their combined scents sending his possessive urges into overdrive. Blindly he reached for her other leg and hoisted that one over his opposite shoulder. He raised himself up, lifting her weight easily and using the wall at her back to steady her. He clamped his mouth over her core and tweaked her clit with his tongue. She jerked and tightened her fists in his hair, pulling it painfully.

"Alex." His name emerged on a strangled sob.

He cupped her ass and dug his tongue inside her channel, sweeping it around and relishing the taste of his seed deep within her.

Vaguely he supposed it was the kinkiest thing he'd ever done — taste his cum in a woman — and he wouldn't have considered it as something he'd ever have wanted to do. But there was something primal about the act, some deep-seated need he had to not only mark Tanvi as his, but also substantiate and pleasure in the fact.

She jerked again and groaned as he thrust his tongue in and out of her, paying special attention to her clit on his withdrawal. He felt it when she was close. Her body stiffened on his shoulders and she made a low whimpering sound, her inner muscles starting to pulse.

He pulled back a little and eyed her opening — it was swollen and glistening with his cum and saliva and her juices. Oh, fuck, he could orgasm just looking at it. He dove forward again, latched on to her clit and sucked. She bucked against him and yelled his name as she came all over his face.

He released Tanvi and sat back on his haunches, gazing up at her from beneath hooded lids. She was sexed up, her face flushed, her chest heaving and her hair tumbling around her shoulders and breasts in a black silk veil. She was gorgeous and she smelled like sex and him — he'd eliminated the jasmine scent altogether.

He was rock-hard again, his cock clamoring for another release and bobbing heavily between his thighs. "Go and get in the bath," he ordered roughly.

As much as he hated washing his scent off her, he'd brand her again in another way. He shook his head, dismayed at the possessive urges that had overtaken him.

He rose to his feet, his erection throbbing painfully. Through the door, he watched Tanvi step gracefully into the warm bath water and settle against the back of the tub, her pink-tipped breasts peeking through the bubbles. His cock quivered in anticipation, his crown already leaking white fluid as he moved to join her.

Chapter Twenty-Five

Tanvi settled at her desk a little gingerly. She was sensitive and sore between her thighs but she enjoyed recalling why.

Never before had a man picked her up and thrust into her like an animal possessed. Alex was so strong. He'd just lifted her and pumped into her from a standing position. Thinking about it made her wet and she clenched her legs together. Hadn't she had enough already?

She blushed as she remembered what Alex had done to her afterward. She should have felt mortified and scandalized at such an act, but she'd embraced it wholeheartedly, had gripped his head and bucked against his mouth like a mad thing. She'd been desperate for the intimacy and the visceral coupling. Alex's mouth on her sex after he'd come inside her was the most erotic thing she'd ever experienced. In fact, she would never even have gone so far as to imagine something like that.

After he'd ordered her into the tub, he'd stalked in behind her. His body had been hard and tight, his abdominals rippling and the sight of his huge erection bobbing under its heavy weight had made her mouth water. He'd stared down at her for a moment, his eyes dilated with lust. Then he'd stepped into the bath in one graceful move, his long legs making easy work of the act. He'd straddled her, his knees either side of her breasts and she'd opened her mouth to him, needing to feel his silky hardness between her lips. He'd groaned, cupped her cheek then taken her invitation and thrust his shaft into her mouth. She'd opened wide, and had tipped her head back for a better angle, relishing the feel and the taste of him. He'd massaged her jaw and eased in farther. Automatically her saliva glands had kicked in and lubricated his erection to ease his glide. He'd murmured to her that he was going to mark her again, that he was going to come down her throat and she'd moaned around his cock.

Tanvi shifted in her chair as her arousal flared and her panties dampened. She shook her head, totally in awe of herself and her newfound, apparently ravenous sexual appetite. She pushed all thoughts aside and reached for the stack of paperwork that had been piled neatly on her desk and got to work.

* * * *

Alex had spent the morning in a meeting with his team and had been brought up to speed on how things were progressing. He was confident that his commercial manager, his chief engineer and his finance manager were asking all the right questions and assessing the information appropriately. They'd hired a local lawyer, skilled in Indian commercial law, and Alex's absence over the past few days had not in any way slowed things down. Having his main team out of head office was something he didn't like to do, but the business in New Delhi was important. Alex knew that if everything worked out as he expected, they'd all be reaping the rewards. Besides, his general manager was handling things in their absence.

Alex had decided to head back to his suite at the Totally Five Star and work on a mountain of other issues that had been awaiting his attention. His assistant and the GM had been dealing with what they could in Alex's absence, but there were a field of matters that he alone had to address.

He leaned back in the comfortable leather seat and plucked a copy of *The Times of India* from the seat back in front. He idly flicked through it, not particularly interested in anything on the pages. Then he came to the social section and his heart skipped a beat. There was an image of Tanvi, looking stunning in a navy blue silk saree, her hazel-green eyes heavily lined in black kohl. But it was the man standing next to her that caught Alex's attention. He was tall and lean with a hard stare and looked to be of a similar age to Tanvi. His arm was banded around her waist and he'd pulled her tightly against him, his fingers digging into the flesh of her hip. *What the fuck?* He looked at the date of the charity function where the photo had been taken and a cold fury swept through him. It was earlier in the week when Tanvi had declined an invitation from him. Now he knew why — she'd been otherwise engaged with another man.

He breathed deeply as his fury mingled with feelings of jealousy and possessiveness. It was clear to Alex that the man in the photo thought of himself as more than a friend. It was the way he'd pulled Tanvi close to his side and the way his fingers dug into her hip possessively. Rage filtered through him. How dare that bastard touch what was his! He gripped the paper tightly and stared blindly out of the window. When had he started thinking of Tanvi as his? It had been a progressive shift, he realized. She'd been slowly working her way under his skin and into his heart and, surprisingly, the sudden understanding didn't terrify him or spur him into running in the opposite direction.

It made him all the more determined, however, to find out who the fuck the guy was and why Tanvi hadn't told him the truth about where she'd been that evening.

Sanjay pulled the car to a stop out the front of the Totally Five Star and Alex exited the vehicle quickly, not waiting for the little driver to open his door. He clutched the offending newspaper page in his hand and stormed through the lobby toward the administration offices.

Tanvi's door was closed and he opened it without knocking. She was hunched over her desk, a sheaf of papers in one hand and an accountant's calculator in the other.

"I won't be a moment, George," she said without looking up.

"It's not George, but when I'm through with you, you'll wish it was," Alex murmured, his tone sinister.

Tanvi started. Alex was looming in the doorway, looking very pissed off, and with some sort of paper gripped in his fist. He narrowed his eyes on her and stalked into the office, closing the door none to quietly behind him.

Her heart jumped into her throat and anxiety snaked down her spine. "What's wrong?"

He drew level with her. "This is what's wrong," he bit out and slammed the paper on the desk.

Tanvi looked down at an image of herself, Rakesh clutching her tightly around the waist. *Fuck*. She didn't swear, but that was the first word that forced its way into her brain.

"It's not how it looks," she murmured. "I can explain."

"Please do," he said, his voice deceptively soft. She knew by the look of him that he was furious, that at any moment his tight control could snap.

"That's Rakesh." She sought frantically for an explanation that would appease him. "He-he's a friend."

"A friend?" Alex scoffed. "He looks a little more than a friend. Do your friends always hold you like that? He may as well have *mine* stamped on his fucking forehead!" He planted his two fists on her desk and leaned forward. "Why didn't you tell me where you were going that night? Why did you lie?"

"I didn't lie," she said hotly, indignation making her bold. "I merely said that I had other plans, which was the truth."

"Other plans meaning you were going on a date." He narrowed his eyes. "Are you fucking him? Has he been inside you, baby?"

"What? No! It's not like that."

Tanvi's mind was reeling. Alex couldn't possibly think that she'd been intimate with Rakesh. She should have felt furious, but the only emotion she could muster was hurt. She was hurt that he'd think so little of her. "I can't believe you would think me capable of that," she said softly.

He glared at her for a moment longer then straightened and shoved both his hands through his hair. "I don't, really," he conceded quietly, dropping his arms to his sides. "I'm just so angry that you wouldn't tell me what you were doing that night. You have to see my side of things. How it would look to me."

Tanvi gazed down at the photo. It definitely appeared like they were more than friends, and she supposed they were, at least to her family. Rakesh even looked a little possessive, she realized with a start. She recalled how he'd grabbed her and tucked her close to his side, remembered vividly the vicious bite of his fingers as he'd dug them into her flesh.

"I do understand how it looks," she murmured. "It was a longstanding social engagement that I couldn't get out of." She waved a hand in the air. "It was for my uncle's benefit, not mine. I didn't want to be there." She pointed at Rakesh's image. "Particularly not with him."

"Who is he?" Alex asked the question she'd been dreading.

Who indeed? It was now or never that she had to come clean.

"He's the man my family wants me to marry."

Chapter Twenty-Six

What the fuck? Alex was floored. Did it mean that Tanvi was engaged to that bastard? The asshole who put his hands on her and declared with his actions that she was his? But then perhaps she was his, at least if her family's wishes figured into anything.

Alex scrubbed his hands through his hair again, aware that now it must be practically standing on end.

"Remind me what year it is? Because going by what you just said, I've got a feeling that we've stepped back in time."

"Arranged marriages are standard practice here."

"So you're going to marry this guy? You're practically engaged?" He was going to lose his shit big time if that was the case.

Tanvi looked down, avoiding his gaze. "It's complicated," she finally mumbled. "My uncle wanted to use the function as a public display that Rakesh and I are together and 'official', but there have been no official arrangements made. Yet."

He breathed a sigh of relief. "Well, if you don't want to marry him, tell your parents that."

She barked a laugh, a sound that held no joy. "It's not that simple."

He lifted her out of her chair and grasped her around the waist, tugging her tight to his body. "You're mine, Tanvi. I'm not having you marry some fucker just because your family wants you to." He looked down at her and the anger he'd felt when he first saw the picture once more took root. "Why have you been deceiving me about this? You've had plenty of opportunities to talk to me about it."

"I didn't know how to explain," she said in a small voice. "And I was assuming that what we were doing was just for a bit of fun." She looked up at him. "You agreed with me on that. This is just a short-term affair."

He narrowed his eyes to slits and growled low in his throat. "It's more than that. Tell me you feel the same way."

"Yes," she finally agreed. "I do feel the same way."

He stared down at her. He wanted to punish her for lying to him and for cheapening what they shared by terming it merely an affair. Later, they could discuss the issues more in depth, but now he needed to show her the consequences for deceiving him.

"Go up to my suite," he demanded, using his Dom's voice. "I'm going to punish you."

"What?"

"You heard me. The longer you linger about it, the harder the punishment will be." He looked at his watch. "It's five o'clock now. You can leave for the day." He took his swipe card from his pocket and pressed it into her hand. "I'll see you up there soon. You know what to do."

She broke his hold and exited the office quickly, head bowed in obedience.

Alex thought about what he'd use on her, prompting his cock to swell and throb in anticipation. He was going to enjoy the fuck out of the next few hours.

* * * *

Once inside Alex's suite, Tanvi hurried to the bedroom, her heart rate kicking with anxious anticipation. Her palms were clammy and her breathing quickened. She was nervous but also strangely excited

She undressed, unwrapping her saree and draping it over the back of a chair. She understood that Alex wanted her naked with her hair down, but she didn't know what to do after that. She removed her underwear and undid her braid, fluffing her fingers through her hair to untangle the thick strands. She thought back to everything she'd read and decided to kneel by the door. Instinctively, she understood that Alex would appreciate the gesture.

Tanvi didn't know how long she waited. It felt like an hour, but she knew it was closer to twenty minutes. She recognized what Alex was doing. This was part of her punishment, making her wait for him, knowing that she'd be anxious with wondering what he was going to do to her.

She heard him enter the suite. The door opened and closed then only silence. She waited on her knees with her head bowed, her hair tumbling over her shoulders to the floor in a black veil. As the silence stretched before her, a shiver worked its way down her spine. She knew he was near, the spicy scent of his aftershave having hit her nose, sending her senses reeling and the subtle shift in the air that always told her he was close.

A soft click sounded in the stillness, then music swelled around them, a song with a deep bass that she hadn't heard before.

Tanvi felt Alex at her back, a soft brush over her shoulder, then his palm grasping her nape and squeezing slightly as he urged her to her feet.

"I'm impressed," he murmured against her ear. "You've been doing your homework."

She remained silent, head bowed, secretly rejoicing that she'd pleased him. She snatched a glimpse of him from beneath her hair and her breath caught. Clad only in his boxers, he screamed everything powerful and masculine. His defined chest and rippling abdominals gleamed under the muted light and she couldn't miss the fact that he was rock hard, his erection straining against the black stretch fabric of his briefs, impressive and huge. The knowledge emboldened her – she was arousing him. That she could produce such a response in him gave her confidence and an odd feminine strength. Her gaze traveled lower to take in his muscular thighs, lightly sprinkled with dark-blond hair, and his bare feet, large but perfectly formed. She smiled to herself and would have giggled had she been allowed. *I even find his feet attractive!*

Alex had needed a moment to compose himself when he first caught sight of Tanvi, kneeling for him, her round backside flush against her heels and that wondrous hair falling around her like a shroud. It was the most erotically sexy thing he'd ever seen and his cock had solidified instantly.

He breathed deeply, standing behind her for a minute, drinking in the sight of her. He'd decided on the way to the suite that he was going to spank her. It was much milder than a paddle or cane and it was more intimate. He wanted to feel her flesh warm under his palm and leave his hand imprint on her lush ass.

He urged her to her feet, grasping her nape as he led her over to the bed. He sat on the edge of the mattress, gripped both her wrists in one hand, and pulled her front first onto his lap, swinging his right leg over her thighs to hold her in place.

"I'm going to spank you. You say your safe word if you have to. But think carefully before you do. It's supposed to hurt a bit. This is a punishment, after all."

"Yes, sir."

She was perfect, so submissive and responsive. "Don't clench either, or I'll make it harder."

Tanvi relaxed into his lap and, when he decided that she was ready, he swung his right hand up and slapped her hard on the ass. She jumped a little then settled back onto his thighs, sighing deeply. He spanked her twice more, his palm on her flesh audible, even over the music. He paused and swept his hand in circles over her reddened cheeks, soothing her a little before continuing. He wouldn't usually be so easy on a submissive, but he found himself wanting to comfort her, even though he was punishing her, an odd and unfamiliar emotion at odds with his usual character. He slapped her again, commencing a steady rhythm, a smack on each ass cheek then one between her thighs Each time his palm made contact with her pussy, she groaned and wriggled against him. He swept his arm under her stomach and tugged her higher so her sex was poised above his cock. He struck her again.

pushing her pussy into his throbbing shaft and prompting a groan from deep in his chest. Her ass cheeks were turning a glowing shade of pink, beautiful against her caramel-colored skin.

"You'll get twenty. We're up to fifteen." He grunted as he spanked her twice more, relishing the sting in his palm.

She whimpered and clutched his calf. He paused, giving her an opportunity to speak her safe word. When she remained silent, he continued, delivering the final three strikes in the triangle configuration, finishing with a swift slap between her thighs. He was breathing heavily, sweat dotting his brow.

"Good girl," he whispered, smoothing his palm across her glowing ass cheeks. "You did really well, baby. You should see your beautiful backside. My fingers are imprinted in your flesh, branding you."

He pushed two fingers into her pussy. *Christ*, she was soaked. He thrust higher and she cried out, trembling and clenching onto his fingers as she came all over him.

"Fuck," he breathed in awe. "You liked your punishment a little too much, sweetness," he murmured, pumping his fingers gently to work her through her orgasm.

He flipped her onto her back and brushed the hair off her forehead. Her eyes were heavy-lidded and her face flushed. The sight of her coming undone in his arms had sent him soaring perilously close to the edge. His cock was a throbbing painfully, the blood pumping so hard that he felt like he had another heartbeat between his legs. He reached between them and shoved his boxers down, anchoring the waistband under his aching balls.

He grasped Tanvi around the waist, lifted her and swung her around so her back was against his front. "Prop yourself up and lift," he ordered between clenched teeth.

She did as he asked and braced herself on his thighs, raising her hips. He grasped the base of his shaft in one hand and squeezed, needing to take the edge off a little. He lined up his erection with her entrance and gripped both her hips, yanking her down while he thrust up.

"Jessuuss," he hissed as he pushed into her wet heat. She felt incredible, swollen and tight after her climax. He'd never fucked without a condom and he was finding his release coming a little too quickly whenever he got inside Tanvi. He had to work hard to maintain his control.

He swept his hand down her belly to between her thighs and located her clit, pressing down with his thumb and sparking a deep moan from her lips. He rubbed the engorged nub and growled into her ear before latching on to the tendon between her neck and shoulder and biting down.

She stiffened, cried his name and jerked against his chest as she trembled and pulsed around his cock. She was amazing and so fucking responsive to him. He needed to come, but he wanted to look into her eyes when he spurted deep inside her. He lifted her again and spun her around to face him.

"Don't close your eyes," he commanded, dropping her onto his steel-hard erection.

She moaned, and he gripped her hips, holding her still and seating himself balls deep in her slick channel. "Don't move," he rasped.

He remained like that, unmoving—his cock locked inside her wet heat as he stared into her eyes. His balls tightened and lust coiled at the base of his spine. Shit, he was going to come. She was close again, the telltale flutters in her core signaling her imminence. This one would border on pain, he thought vaguely — she'd be overly sensitive and swollen. He released her hip and pinched her nipple hard. She gasped, jerked and opened her eyes wide in surprise as a third orgasm swept through her. She gripped his cock like a vise and milked him, little whimpers erupting from her parted lips. It was enough to trigger his own climax and he came violently, an intense feeling of pleasure rocketing through him as he emptied himself inside her. Christ, he hadn't even moved, there'd been no thrusting or pumping, no driving of hips or meeting of mouths, just the delicious feel of Tanvi's pussy, clenching his cock rhythmically until he exploded.

Chapter Twenty-Seven

Alex wrapped his arms around Tanvi as she slumped against him in exhaustion. He remained buried inside her, unwilling to break the connection.

He stood, cupping her backside, and walked to the bathroom. He bent, using one hand to turn on the taps, then poured a generous slug of patchouli-scented bubble bath under the running water, aromatic steam rising to envelop them. He turned and looked at the full-length mirror and at Tanvi's round ass cupped by his hands, red finger marks crossing her flesh, her hair falling to just above the crack of her butt and her head resting on his shoulder. Arousal hit him like a sledgehammer and he swelled inside her, ready for round two.

When the water was deep enough, he stepped into the tub and lowered them under the bubbles. He bent his knees and urged Tanvi back against them. She smiled sleepily at him. "Is your new favorite place inside me?"

He smirked. "It's been my favorite place since the first time I fucked you."

"Such a charmer." She smiled.

Alex lathered soap between his hands and started to massage her breasts, cupping the plump mounds and kneading then smoothing his palms over her nipples. She threw her head back. "Oh yes, please."

He massaged her for a moment longer, delighting in the heaviness of her breasts and her tight little nipples. She really was designed for sex. She was voluptuous, sensual and a perfect handful. He could lift her easily, which was ideal for manipulating her where he wanted her. His cock swelled larger, thumping in time with his rapid heartbeat. He brushed his palm down her tummy to her sex and fingered her clit, prompting a gasp from her.

"Sensitive?"

"Yes," she murmured, gazing at him from beneath heavy lids. "But it's not really bad."

He chuckled. "You don't want me to stop?"

She shook her head. "No, please don't."

"You're insatiable, baby." He lathered more soap between his hands and smoothed them down her sides, using his thumbs to part her pussy lips and locate her clit under its hood. She moaned and gyrated her hips.

"Stay still," he ordered. "I want to come like I did before. Buried deep within you, with just the feel of your tight cunt clenching around me."

She stilled, her eyes sparking at his crude words.

"Touch your tits. Play with them."

She hesitated.

"Do it," he barked.

Slowly, she drew her hands up her sides and cupped her breasts, kneading and massaging the heavy mounds. Her lips parted and she whimpered. He loved the little sounds she made.

"That's it, baby. See how good you feel?"

He circled her clit with his index finger then pressed the little bundle of nerves. She gasped and closed her eyes, pinching each of her nipples and pulling them taut.

"Fuck yes," he rasped. "Make it hurt, sweetness."

She tugged harder, her nipples elongating and stretching.

He massaged her clit faster, rubbing and tweaking the nub until he felt her insides stir and tighten. His balls pulled up and pleasure bloomed deep in his gut.

"I'm gonna come," he ground between clenched teeth.

His cock pulsed and kicked, and she clamped around him, gripping him like a fist, her inner muscles undulating wildly.

"Arghh!" she cried, stiffening on top of him and staring deep into his eyes, her body trembling.

He sat up, clamped his mouth on her neck and sucked hard as his release barreled down on him. He wrapped his arms around her waist and kept his mouth locked to her neck, blasts of pleasure rocketing through him.

Alex released Tanvi's neck and slumped back against the tub, Tanvi coming with him, her body a dead weight on his chest. He picked up the bath sponge and dribbled water down her spine as their breathing started to slow and regulate. Finally, he urged her back a little and assessed her. She was flushed from her orgasm and the warm bath, her eyelids heavy, the tips of her hair swirling in the water around them. She had a deep red mark on her neck where he'd sucked her. He liked it.

"I'm sorry. I've given you a love bite, but I like my mark on you," he murmured. "Let's rinse off and I'll put you to bed."

* * * *

Tanvi lay face down on the bed where Alex had placed her after their bath. The sheets were smooth and cool against her sensitized skin. She felt incredibly lethargic and sleepy.

Alex squirted cool cream on her backside and smoothed his palm across her tender cheeks.

"Your ass looks so good right now," he murmured. "Pink, with my hand marks imprinted on your flesh."

She moaned, warmth blooming in her lower belly. She couldn't possibly be turned on again. She barely had enough energy to lift her head. But as Alex continued massaging her ass with that cool cream, her core quickened and her pussy moistened in arousal. A sliver of fear worked its way under her skin. That last orgasm she'd had had bordered on pain and had been more of an ache than a release and she was worried that another so close to the last would feel even more intense.

She wriggled involuntarily, pushing her sex into the mattress in an attempt to relieve the longing throbs that had flared low in her belly.

Alex chuckled. "Turned on again, baby? You really are insatiable. I like that. I love that you're so responsive to me." He gripped her ass cheeks and squeezed, inciting a gasp from low in her throat. "This was supposed to be a punishment," he mused, continuing to squeeze and knead her ass. "But it's turned into an orgasm fest for you. Perhaps your chastisement will have to come later."

She heard a rustling sound then the mattress shifted and a lid snapped open, followed by liquid dribbling between her thighs. *Lubricant?*

"I know you're wet, sweetness, but you'll be very sensitive. Your pussy will be swollen and tender. This will help."

He caressed her folds softly, smoothing the cooling lubricant over her sex and pushing some inside.

She moaned and undulated her hips, relishing the twinge of pain as Alex penetrated her with his fingers.

"I'm going to fuck you from behind and come all over your ass," he said gruffly.

The mattress dipped and she felt him on the bed next to her. Then he was grasping her around the waist and lifting her to her knees.

She gripped the sheets and jutted her ass out, waiting. Finally, he clutched her hips and pushed into her. She stiffened a moment as he worked his thick cock into her swollen channel. Finally, he was seated to the hilt and she relaxed, breathing deeply through a twinge of pain.

"Are you okay?" he asked, his voice tight.

"Yes, I'm fine." She was tender and sore but she couldn't deny that she wanted him again.

He started to move, drawing out slowly and dragging his cock piercing through her sensitive folds before thrusting in deeply.

She moaned and pushed back to meet each of his languorous drives, pleasure and pain coalescing in her lower belly. He released one of her hips and snaked a hand down her abdomen to between her thighs. His fingers were wet with lubricant and slid over her outer folds before he located her clit and pressed. She jerked and gasped, slivers of sensation radiating outward. She didn't think she could orgasm again, but she loved having him inside her.

He smoothed his other hand up to her left breast and squeezed the mound roughly, thrusting into her again on a deep lunge. He had one hand on her clit and the other on her breast and was using both to manipulate her body back and forth on his cock.

Her insides started to tingle, the dull throb inside morphing into a pleasurable ache. "Oh, yes," she breathed. Perhaps she *could* manage one more.

He thrust harder and faster, his balls slapping her pussy on each plunge.

She gulped and whimpered. "I'm going to come *again*."

"Good girl" he rasped. "I want to feel you climax all over my cock."

She held her breath as the sensations gathered and merged, swirling and coiling into a tight ball of pressure.

He grasped her breast harder, pinching her nipple with his thumb and forefinger, and that's all it took. The sharp jab of pain mixed with the building pleasure sent her tumbling into a tumultuous orgasm. She gasped then stiffened, whimpering softly as her insides undulated in an aching wave.

He released her breast and gripped both her hips, thrusting three more times, grunting and growling like an animal.

Then she was empty and his cock was pressed against her ass. He groaned deep in his throat and she felt warm ribbons of cum shoot over her backside.

He stayed like that for a moment, clutching her hips and breathing heavily. "Damn," he finally grated.

"That looks so hot, my cum on your ass, over my finger marks. I'm going to let it dry like that."

She slumped to her stomach in exhaustion, vaguely registering Alex getting off the bed. She heard him pad over to the suite phone, then he was talking to Deepak, ordering dinner and reminding him of her peanut allergy. That was the last thing she heard before she slipped into a deep sleep.

Chapter Twenty-Eight

Alex looked at his watch — seven-thirty. He should wake Tanvi for dinner. He crossed the room to where she still lay on her stomach on the bed, her hair spread out like a beautiful Spanish fan over the pillows. He looked down at her. His cum had dried in thick ribbons on her caramel-colored skin. The redness had faded but his finger imprints were still visible. He caressed her ass cheeks, marveling at the erotic picture she made, then he knelt on the floor beside the bed and brushed her hair back from her forehead.

"Tanvi, baby. Wake up."

She moaned and tried to burrow into the mattress.

He chuckled. "Come on, you have to get up. Dinner's here and we need to talk."

She huffed and flopped onto her back. "What time is it?"

"Seven-thirty. Why don't you freshen up and I'll see you in the dining room."

Groaning, Tanvi sat up and swung her legs off the bed. Alex chuckled and handed her a gown.

"Are you sore, sweetness?"

She scowled at him. "What do you think?" she muttered petulantly. "You had your way with me over and over again. My insides feel rubbed raw."

"I'm glad you're sore," he said seriously. "That was supposed to be a punishment after all and besides" — he smirked — "you'll remember where I've been and what I've done to you."

She rolled her eyes and shrugged into the hotel's waffle fabric gown. "You really are kinky," she muttered as she shuffled through to the bathroom, then closed the door behind her.

Alex smiled. His Tanvi obviously had a tendency to wake up on the wrong side of the bed. He grabbed the food tray that Deepak had organized earlier and arranged the plates on the dining room table. Selecting Opeth's *Damnation* album on his iPod, he then opened a crisp white wine that had been chilling in a wine bucket. He'd just finished placing plates and cutlery on the table when Tanvi appeared. She'd brushed her hair and twisted it into a side braid that hung over one shoulder. Her freshly scrubbed face glowed and a soft floral scent drifted around her.

He looked her over appreciatively and pulled a chair out. "Sit."

Tanvi sat and Alex took a seat opposite.

"I ordered a Greek salad. I thought we'd have something light." He picked up Tanvi's plate and served her a generous portion of salad. "Wine?"

"Please." She smiled.

Alex served himself then poured them each a glass. "Shall we toast to us this time?" he murmured, raising his goblet.

"To us," Tanvi agreed, clinking her glass with his.

They ate quietly, each lost in their own thoughts. Alex was trying to work out how to tactfully broach the subject of Tanvi's pseudo-engagement and eventually decided on the straightforward approach. He recognized that the subject was not a pleasant one for her, but they had to discuss it.

He put his knife and fork down and cleared his throat. "What exactly is your relationship status with this guy you were with the other night? You said that there's nothing official. What does that mean?"

She sighed and took a sip of wine then replaced the glass with care by her plate. "It's complicated," she eventually muttered.

Alex cursed quietly. "You said that earlier and it's not a good enough explanation. I think I deserve more than that." He studied her over the rim of his glass. She was staring down at her plate, fiddling with her knife and biting her lower lip.

Finally, she looked up at him. "As I said, arranged marriages are standard practice in India. It's the way we do things, but not everyone is happy with...their family's choices for them."

"And what are the things that constitute a good marriage" — he waved a hand in the air — "according to your family?"

She sighed again, the sound so forlorn and dejected that his heart constricted.

"They consider many things — the man's family, their standing in society, religion, caste, money, even the date and time of birth and whether that predicts a good and prosperous match."

Fuck, it sounded more like negotiating a business merger than a life union.

"Haven't you read the Matrimonials in the paper?" she continued. "Where people advertise for marriage partners? They always give a list of requirements they want from applicants."

Alex recalled reading that section and being astounded at the preferences listed to the point where he wondered exactly how many people would meet the stringent requirements. "What about dowries?" he questioned. "I thought they were illegal."

"They *are* illegal." She shrugged. "But it's hard to police and easily circumvented by the female's family, stating that what could be considered a dowry is merely a gift for their daughter's use. Many families still expect a dowry from the girl's family and often the demands grow and don't stop with what was given at the time of marriage."

"Has a dowry been offered to this man?"

"Probably, but I'm not privy to the details."

"And what does your family get out of the union?"

Tanvi hesitated. "I'm not sure, but I think it has something to do with my uncle, my mother's brother. The man they want me to marry, Rakesh, his family is quite prominent in the community, particularly in political circles, and I believe my uncle has designs on a political position. Also, my father said that if the marriage goes ahead, Rakesh's father would send business his way."

Alex rubbed a hand over his jaw. "Why does your uncle have so much sway?"

She laughed coldly. "My father seems to do whatever my uncle wants of him. Don't get me wrong, I love my father, but he's a weak man where my uncle's concerned and I have no idea why." She paused, looking thoughtful. "I think it might have something to do with some misplaced sense of loyalty. When my paternal grandfather died, my uncle automatically assumed the head of the household. My mother was still young at the time, but before his death, her father had approved a marriage to my father. I don't know the details, but I suspect my uncle only allowed the prearranged marriage to go ahead under certain conditions. I guess this might be where my father's reticence to go against my uncle's wishes comes from."

Alex's brain was running a hundred miles an hour, processing all the information that Tanvi had just imparted. It was like a different world. The culture and the traditions were so alien to him but he had to respect their societal values. He couldn't, however, respect the fact that Tanvi could be forced into a marriage that she didn't want. Of course, it was also best for his self-interest that Tanvi not marry, but, more importantly, what did *she* want? He forced himself to ask the next question, telling himself that he wouldn't become angry if he didn't like the answer.

"Do you want to marry this man, Rakesh?"

"No!" She shuddered and wrapped her arms around herself. "He's not a nice person. He can be cruel and quite vicious. In fact, I can think of nothing worse than spending the rest of my life with him."

Alex was reassured by her adamant response, but equally pissed off that she'd been put in such an invidious position. What sort of loving family put their own desires before those of their daughter? No wonder she'd been so grave and unhappy when he'd first met her. She'd been marking time until she had to enter into a union with a man she despised.

He clenched his jaw. "What happens if you refuse to marry him?"

She looked up, wide-eyed. "My family would disown me," she whispered.

Tanvi watched a range of emotions pass over Alex's features — disbelief, astonishment then rage. She saw it clearly. His eyes narrowed and flashed and a muscle ticked in his tensed jaw.

"Are you fucking serious?" he finally muttered, his voice ominously low.

"I-I think so," she stammered, then hastened to add, "but we haven't discussed it. It's just that my father keeps talking to me about it… He's anxious for me to agree to the marriage and, if I keep stalling, he's threatened to go ahead and make the arrangements with or without my consent. He told me that he's only delayed this long out of deference to my mother…and me, apparently. But his patience with me has run out. He told me so the other night."

Alex scrubbed a hand through his hair, a faraway look in his eyes. "Right," he finally announced, his voice all business. "I need to think about this."

"Think about what?" Tanvi asked, incredulous. "There's nothing to think about. It is what it is. Now you know why I've been so reticent to take things more seriously with you. It's impossible. I have to accept that this is my lot in life, this is what awaits me." She tried hard to maintain her composure, but her bottom lip started trembling. "I just wanted something for me," she whispered. "The things you make me feel are like nothing I've ever experienced before. I wanted…something to remember, a relationship, however brief, that I could look back on and reminisce about. A sweet memory to keep me going through what I expect to be a lot of dark days ahead of me."

Alex glared at her. "I thought you were stronger than this, Tanvi. I didn't expect you to be the sort of woman to accept something you don't agree with, to unquestioningly enter into a situation that is so abhorrent to you."

Tanvi narrowed her eyes on him, suddenly furious with him for calling her out on her lack of courage, on her failure to go against her parents. "Didn't you?" she sneered, injecting as much venom as she could into the words. "What do you think I've been doing with you?" As soon as the words were out of her mouth, she wished them back in, but it was too late. Alex, who had been glaring at her, sat back as if she'd slapped him.

"That's how you feel, then," he said, his voice flat. "I'm glad you've finally told me. I didn't realize what we were doing was so abhorrent to you. "

"No! No!" she cried, vehemently trying to backpedal. "I'm sorry. I didn't mean it." She leaned across the table and grasped his hand. "I was angry at what you just said."

He gently extricated his hand from hers and pushed himself away from the table. "There's generally a little truth in what people say, even in anger."

Tanvi shot up from her seat and raced around to Alex's side of the table. She knelt before him. "Please, Alex. I didn't mean it at all. I was upset that you so easily and clearly saw through me. Saw through to my cowardice and weakness, and I had the sudden urge to hurt you for it." She dropped her forehead to his knees.

"Please believe me. I told you before how much this time with you has meant to me. I've loved everything we've done together. I've enjoyed every minute." She took a shuddering breath, suddenly overwhelmed by the entire situation. Overwhelmed by her feelings for Alex and the seemingly impossible state of affairs with Rakesh and her family.

Alex stroked her hair, his touch so soft she barely felt it. "Perhaps we need some time out," he muttered tonelessly. "I think a little space will do us both good."

She peered up at him, not trying anymore to stem the flow of tears that had been threatening for the last half hour. "I'll go," she whispered brokenly, picking herself up off the floor.

She made her way to the bedroom and dressed in record time, suddenly needing desperately to get away from Alex and the mess she'd made of everything. She picked up her handbag, walked to the door and, opening it quietly, she slipped through, hoping fervently that it wouldn't be for the last time.

Chapter Twenty-Nine

Tanvi had tossed and turned all night, replaying the scene with Alex. Surely he'd understand that what she'd said had only been said in anger and fear. She'd wanted to lash out at him for seeing her weakness and because she was scared. Scared of losing him and terrified about what her future entailed. It hadn't helped that her father had given her the third degree when she'd returned home, wanting to know where she'd been spending all her time and with whom. She'd been quite pleased with herself when she'd stood up to him and told him in no uncertain terms that she was an adult and, as such, far beyond having to inform her parents of her every move. Her father had been so surprised he'd been struck speechless, which was the only decent outcome of the previous night.

She moved sluggishly as she got ready for work, washing and drying her hair until it hung in a thick, shiny curtain down her back. Perhaps she'd cut it — she could make an appointment for this afternoon. It took her so long to get it dry that the thought of being able to just fluff it and go was very appealing. *Why not?* She didn't think Alex would be around to object. She was applying her makeup when she suddenly remembered that she was meeting Riya for their standard Friday morning breakfast at the Totally Five Star restaurant and a chat with her best friend was probably just what she needed. Riya's frankness and open-mindedness would be a welcome relief.

Tanvi opened her wardrobe and scanned the contents. She wanted something to make her feel feminine and strong, sexy but professional.

An hour later, she walked into the Totally Five Star Hotel restaurant. Riya was waiting for her, a pot of tea and some pastries on the table in front of her. Tanvi felt so relieved to see her friend that tears pricked her eyes as she walked toward her.

Riya jumped up and enveloped her in a hug. "What's wrong?" she cried. "What's happened?"

Tanvi hugged her back then settled into a seat at the table, ready to get everything off her chest in the hopes that Riya could provide some much-needed advice.

* * * *

Alex was in a foul mood and the phone call to Australia at three a.m. hadn't improved his demeanor. The last conversation with Tanvi had been playing on rerun through his mind. In truth, he knew that what she'd said, she'd said out of her fear and anger but he couldn't deny that it had fucking pissed him off, and if he were honest, even hurt him a little. Fuck, this woman was turning him into such a pussy. He couldn't recall ever being remotely concerned about what a woman thought of him in the past. Of course, he'd always treated women respectfully, but he'd never been hurt by one before and the emotion was disconcerting.

He'd also been trying to get his head around what she'd told him about the arranged marriage business. It wasn't a tradition that he understood but he had to appreciate Tanvi's position in the situation and think about how the fuck he was going to fix it for her.

He strode toward the restaurant where he was meeting Jay for a morning coffee and stopped dead on the threshold when he saw Tanvi. His breath caught at the sight of her, her hair, which she usually wore in a braid for work, she'd left flowing and shiny down her back. She was selecting fruit from the buffet and her tight pencil skirt cupped her ass like a pair of greedy hands. When she turned, he got a glimpse of her generous cleavage, her breasts swaying slightly under the soft silk of her blue blouse. A group of businessmen at a nearby table were ogling her blatantly, spurring an involuntary, possessive growl to emanate from deep in his chest. The need to step forward and claim her as his warred with the need to punish her for hurting him. He took a deep breath, closed his eyes for a beat and turned toward the lobby. He'd forgotten that Tanvi met Riya on Fridays for breakfast and, even though he'd practically forgiven her for using him as her whipping post, he wasn't ready to see her just yet.

He hit speed dial on his phone. "Jay, it's Alex. I'll meet you in the lobby for that coffee."

He chose a secluded corner and sat to wait for his friend to join him. A couple of minutes later, Jay strode over, looking every bit the manager of a five-star hotel in a bespoke suit and silk Armani tie. He rose to meet him, exchanging a handshake and a back slap.

"Mate, it's good to see you," Alex greeted him. "I need to pick your brains about arranged marriages."

Jay looked surprised. "Really?" he laughed. "You never cease to amaze me. I'll order our coffees and you can fill me in on what's been happening."

* * * *

Tanvi took a bite of a pastry. It was sweet and crunchy, but there was a taste to it that was disconcerting. There was also a thick, cinnamon icing on top, which was new. They were normally served plain. She'd just finished telling Riya about everything that had happened since they'd caught up, and Riya had been hanging on her every word, interjecting every now and again with a question, usually about the BDSM aspect of what Alex had introduced her to. Riya was fascinated and, she admitted, quite jealous of Tanvi's sexual exploits.

"You know," Riya pointed at her. "A week ago you wouldn't have dreamed of talking about any of this stuff. You would have blushed and told me to mind my own business. Now you're practically a sexpert!"

Tanvi giggled. "Hardly, although I have to admit Alex made me feel things I didn't think were possible."

"Don't do the past tense, Tanvi. I'm sure Alex will get over what you said last night."

Tanvi sighed. "Even if he does, it can't go anywhere. I might as well get accustomed to that fact sooner rather than later." She nibbled on her pastry. There was that taste again and she started to feel odd, her mouth tingling.

"Tanvi! Tanvi, are you okay?" She heard Riya's voice like she was speaking through a tunnel.

"I feel strange," Tanvi slurred. Why did she sound drunk? She tried desperately to speak properly, but her throat felt tight and she was finding it difficult to breathe. She scratched at her neck, the sudden itch seeming unbearable.

"Tanvi, sweetheart, you're scaring me." Riya was in front of her now, holding her by the shoulders. Tanvi tried to focus on her friend, but a sudden cramp pierced her stomach and she doubled over in pain.

Alex and Jay had just finished their coffee when a disturbance in the restaurant had them jumping up from their chairs and running to investigate. They skidded to a stop at the entrance and Alex took in the scene. Tanvi was on the floor, Riya crouched next to her and yelling for assistance while restaurant patrons hovered ineffectually nearby.

Alex sprinted over to them, his heart in his mouth and Jay fast on his heels. Vaguely, he registered his friend talking to someone urgently on the phone.

"Alex! Thank God," Riya cried when she saw him. "Something's wrong with her."

Alex crouched next to Riya and assessed Tanvi. She was wheezing in obvious distress and a red rash was developing on her chest and neck.

"She's allergic to peanuts," Alex barked. "She's having an allergic reaction. Does she have an epinephrine injector?" He looked at Riya.

"I don't know," she cried, wringing her hands. "She doesn't have her bag with her."

"Jay! We need a doctor. Now!"

"I've called him. He's here in the hotel and on his way."

A moment later, there was movement at the doorway and a man in a white doctor's gown rushed in, a couple of nurses quick on his heel and wheeling a gurney.

The doctor shooed everyone out of the way and knelt next to Tanvi. He checked her vital signs. "She needs adrenaline," he announced briskly, placing an oxygen mask over her mouth. "Get her to the medical center now."

The nurses loaded her onto the gurney and raced out of the restaurant, the doctor keeping pace and monitoring Tanvi's breathing and heart rate.

Alex willed himself not to follow. He didn't want to be in the way and he knew they'd work more efficiently without distractions. He sat back on his heels, shoving a shaky hand through his hair. Fuck, he had enough adrenaline for the both of them pumping through his veins. "Where are they taking her?" he croaked. "I need to be with her."

"To the medical center here at the hotel. I'll show you the way."

"I'm coming with you," Riya interjected.

Alex nodded and got to his feet to follow Jay, who was already moving in the direction the medical team had gone. "You have a medical center?" Alex asked as they walked briskly toward the elevators.

"Yes, we also employee two doctors and four nurses, so there's always someone on duty or on call. The center is well equipped. They'll have everything they need to treat her appropriately." Jay looked at Alex. "It gives our guests peace of mind. Many are concerned about going to an Indian hospital. We can't perform major surgery, of course, but it's suitable for minor injuries and to monitor patients."

"I can't understand how it happened," Riya whispered. "She eats that pastry because it's made specifically for food intolerances."

Alex and Jay shared a look as they entered the elevator. Jay punched the button for the first floor. "The medical center is on the same level as the Totally Five Star spa. It takes up the entire south-west corner."

The elevator dinged their arrival and they exited, following Jay down the passageway to a door at the end. Jay rang the bell. A moment later, the door was opened by one of the nurses and they were ushered inside.

Alex looked around. They were in what looked to be a standard doctor's office. There were two doors leading off it to other areas that Alex assumed were where the longer-term patients stayed.

"I'll leave you here," Jay murmured, slapping Alex on the back. "I need to investigate how an apparently non-allergenic food item became contaminated. We'll have to stop serving those pastries immediately. I'll check in later."

"This way," the nurse indicated, leading them through to another room.

Tanvi lay on a hospital bed covered by a thick, white blanket and hooked up to a heart monitor. Alex rushed over to her side and grasped one of her hands in his. She looked so fragile and vulnerable lying in the large bed, her thick black eyelashes fanned out on her cheeks, her once ruby red lips now pale.

"She's stable," the doctor said from his position by the bed. "She needs rest. Her blood pressure dropped, but we've stabilized it. We're monitoring her vital signs to be on the safe side. I expect the worst is over, however."

He replaced the clipboard he'd been scribbling on. "I'll give you some privacy."

Alex and Riya took seats by Tanvi's side. Alex rubbed his thumb over the back of her hand, caressing in soothing circles. He looked across at Riya. "How did she come to eat peanuts? She's always so careful."

Riya shook her head. "I don't know. As I said before, she always eats the same type of pastry because she knows it's safe."

"Are you sure she didn't confuse it with something else?"

Riya shook her head. "I'm positive. They're a particular shape, different from the others, and they're always labeled."

Alex's mind was racing. The snake incident and now this. It was too much of a coincidence for his liking and, after what he'd just discovered about her personal life, he didn't think it was too much of a stretch to assume that someone was targeting her — trying to hurt her. He clenched his jaw in anger. Fuck, God help the person when Alex got his hands on them.

"She's waking up," Riya whispered.

He looked down at Tanvi as her eyes fluttered open.

"Alex?" She looked down her body and struggled to sit up. "What's going on?"

"Shh, stay still," he soothed. "You're in the medical center at the hotel. You had an allergic reaction. It's okay, I'm here."

Her eyes widened then, to his horror, she started to cry.

Chapter Thirty

Tanvi's mind felt like fog — trying to recognize what was going on was like trying to wade through quicksand. Where was she? And why was she so tired? She felt like she could sleep for a week. She heard voices speaking softly — about her. She had to open her eyes, but her eyelids felt so heavy. Finally, she got them to obey and she fluttered her eyelids open, her gaze alighting immediately on Alex. She struggled to sit up, but he shushed her and urged her back down, saying something about an allergic reaction. It was all too much and, unbearably, she started to cry. She struggled to regain control of herself, but fat tears continued to stream down her cheeks and the harder she tried to stop them, the harder they fell.

She looked to her right and saw Riya, sitting next to her bed.

"Oh, sweetie, don't cry!" Riya grasped her hand and squeezed. "You've had a shock. You're okay now."

Tanvi scrubbed at her face, taking deep breaths. She remembered now, they'd been in the restaurant eating breakfast when she'd started to feel strange, but what happened afterward was just a blur.

"I'll go." She heard Alex's low voice and recalled with a start that he was in the room with them.

"No!" She turned toward him and grasped his arm. "Please, don't go."

"I thought my being here was making you upset," he murmured, sitting back down.

"No, it's as Riya said. I've just had a shock."

Riya stood and dropped a kiss to her forehead. "I'm so glad you're okay. You scared the life out of me, lady! I've got to get to work, but I'll call you later." She winked. "I'll leave you in Alex's capable hands."

Tanvi glanced at Alex. He looked drawn and apprehensive, his hair sticking out at all angles, telling her that he'd been yanking at it. He was worried about her and the realization sent a warm glow flaring in her belly. She reached a shaky hand out to trace the scar along his cheek.

"Why the hell didn't you have your handbag with you?" he snarled and the warm glow vanished.

She snatched her hand back. "I left it in my office. I didn't think—"

"No, you didn't think," he snapped. "Christ, Tanvi, you could have died!"

Her bottom lip started to tremble and she felt the onslaught of fresh tears. *Oh, hell, what's wrong with me?*

Immediately, Alex rested his elbows on the bed next to her and grasped her hand. "I'm sorry," he whispered. "You just scared the hell out of me and I'm not handling it very well."

"It's okay," she mumbled. "I understand."

He closed his eyes and breathed deeply. "Why didn't you have your bag with you?" he asked again in a softer tone.

"I've never needed my injector so I forget sometimes. The few times I've had an allergic reaction, it's just consisted of hives and nausea. I've never had such a severe response and I'm always careful. The pastry I was eating this morning is one I always eat because I know it doesn't contain nuts. In fact, it's made specifically for allergy sufferers. That's why I like to eat here at the hotel — they cater for food intolerances." She paused. "This time, though, it had a thick cinnamon icing on it, which was different."

Alex didn't want to broach the concern uppermost in his mind. It had to be addressed, however. He wasn't a drama queen by any stretch, but the more he thought about the snake in their suite and now the allergy incident, the more he believed they weren't accidental occurrences. He needed to raise his concerns with Tanvi, if for nothing else than to ensure that she'd be careful, at least until they could work out who was behind it.

He squeezed her hand. "Tanvi, who knows about your allergy?"

"Well, it's not a secret and most people remember because peanut allergies are not common here in India. It's pretty standard that I inform restaurants or function centers, wherever I have to eat, that I'm allergic. Like I said, this is the most severe reaction I've had."

He chose his next words carefully. "Don't you think it's strange...first the snake on the train and now this?"

She raised her eyebrows. "You think someone has deliberately tried to hurt me?"

"I can't be sure, but I don't like coincidences. Riya told me that you always eat the same pastry at breakfast. It wouldn't be hard for someone to tamper with it, or pay someone to tamper with it. You just said that the icing was new and heavily flavored with cinnamon, perhaps to disguise the taste. There's a lot of staff here, coming and going, and breakfast is one of their busiest times."

She frowned, biting her bottom lip. "Isn't it rather extreme? That snake in our suite could have easily killed one or both of us. And I know that peanut allergies can be deadly if the reaction is severe enough and anaphylactic shock results. That's why my doctor was adamant that I keep an epinephrine injector. Even though my few attacks have been limited to hives and nausea, he said that reactions can vary and it's not worth taking the risk."

"I've done some investigation about the snake. Apparently Indian kraits are relatively docile during the day, even when provoked. It's at night when they become more active and most of the literature indicates that they don't tend toward immediate attack but generally only when they feel threatened."

"What are you suggesting?"

"I think that perhaps the snake was planted to scare you, or us, and it wasn't meant to kill. Still, it's a pretty risky fucking scare tactic, particularly as the thing is venomous—no one could predict what a snake would do. Perhaps whoever planted it didn't realize that we would be spending the night on the train. Maybe they expected that a coiled, docile serpent would put the scare of God into whoever found it—I don't know. Or they just might not have cared if someone died as a result. And you said yourself that the few reactions you've had to peanuts resulted in nothing more alarming than an irritating skin condition. Perhaps if someone did tamper with the pastry, it was with the intent to cause you an unsightly rash and not to kill you."

She looked troubled, her frown deepening. "But who knew we were going to Agra and when?"

"The hotel, of course, and Sanjay. He wouldn't do anything deliberately to put us in danger, but if someone asked him an innocuous question about my movements, he'd probably answer." He sighed and rubbed his jaw, which had started to ache from the tension. "Look, I'm going to chat to Jay about this and see if he has any suggestions. I don't want you alone at the moment. I'll speak to George and see if you can take some of your work to my suite. No one can get in without a security swipe card and I'll ensure that Deepak will be there with you."

"Is that really necessary?"

"I think it is. Just until I do some investigation and try to determine if this was a deliberate attack."

"Okay," she eventually acquiesced. "I guess you're right."

He stood and gave her a chaste kiss. "You get some rest. I imagine your body needs time to recover from such a shock to the system. I'll ask the doctor to inform me when you're cleared to leave. I'll come and get you and take you to the rooms."

Alex made his way quickly to Jay's office. He wanted to see if his friend had had any success in discovering what had happened that morning at breakfast.

Chapter Thirty-One

Tanvi sank back into the pillows. She really was exhausted, but her mind was refusing to let her sleep. She'd been thinking about what Alex had said and, reluctantly, she had to admit that he might have a point. She didn't want to believe it, but she'd had a niggling concern that she hadn't given voice to after the incident with the snake. That occurrence had seemed too strange to dismiss completely. Now there were the nuts in the pastry. She had a standing date with Riva each Friday morning at the restaurant, so it wouldn't take a private investigator to work out where she'd be and what she'd be eating. Could it be her uncle? Could he be so callous and ruthless to succeed? She knew enough about politics to know that her uncle could just grease the palms of a few people in the right places to get a step ahead. But perhaps it was the introductions to those right people that he was looking for. After all, it wasn't *what* you knew but *who* you knew.

Her mind wandered to Rakesh. She couldn't believe that he'd be behind it. She didn't think he even liked her that much and definitely not enough to go to all the trouble of threatening her. She couldn't understand it. None of it made sense.

* * * *

Alex finished explaining his concerns to Jay and was gratified when his friend agreed with him.

"I think you're right to be concerned, Alex. I would have been surprised by the appearance of a snake on any train. But at the risk of sounding conceited, I'd like to think that it would be impossible for a snake to slither onto the Totally Five Star carriages without being noticed. The suites are meticulously checked to ensure that everything is in order, so the only way I believe a snake went undetected was because whoever planted it there intended it that way. Also, Indian kraits are not often found in highly populated areas. I think I can safely say that it wasn't an accident. I received the report from the staff this morning and that's why I wanted to meet you for coffee."

Alex pushed a hand through his hair. "Well, I've told you everything I know, which isn't much. I need to get to the bottom of this."

Jay sat forward in his chair. "It might seem difficult to comprehend. Situations like this don't often occur in the West, but this is India..." He shrugged. "I have a vested interest in finding out who's behind these incidences. I'd help you, because you're my friend, but now that someone has put the safety of my guests at risk and therefore the reputation of the hotel, this has become a top priority for me. I've thought about contacting the police with this, but I think they'll tell us they don't have anything definitive to point to a deliberate attack, as both incidences could be considered accidents. Also a bunch of police swarming around the hotel is something I'd like to avoid and, to be perfectly honest, they don't move particularly fast. I think we'll have better luck making some quiet enquiries." He rubbed his jaw thoughtfully. "I know a lot of people in the right places," he continued. "These people run in similar circles to Tanvi and Rakesh and their families. I'll have a quiet chat with some of them and see if they can tell me anything more."

"That sounds like a reasonable place to start," Alex agreed. "I'm going to talk to Sanjay. I want to know if anyone has been asking questions about my movements."

They each stood and shook hands. "I'll check in with you tomorrow," Jay said as he walked Alex to the door. "We'll regroup again then."

As soon as Alex left Jay's office, he received a phone call from the hotel doctor informing him that Tanvi was well enough to leave the medical center. When he arrived to pick her up, she was sitting in the doctor's office, waiting for him.

He squatted by her side. "How are you feeling?"

She smiled. "Much better, thank you. I feel back to normal."

He grasped her hand and helped her to her feet. "Good. We'll stop by your desk and pick up some of your work, then I'll settle you in the suite."

* * * *

An hour later, Tanvi was sitting in front of her laptop in Alex's rooms. She still wasn't sure if it was entirely necessary but she hadn't argued. She supposed it was better to be safe than sorry and George had no problems with her working out of the office.

She worked quietly for a few hours, Deepak popping in from time to time to ask if she needed anything. At one o'clock, the little valet brought her in a cup of tea and a chicken salad sandwich. She smiled her thanks, suddenly feeling ravenous, and took a break to eat her lunch.

She'd just finished her sandwich when a knock sounded at the door. She thought nothing of it until raised voices invaded the suite, growing closer to where she'd stationed herself at the desk in the sitting room. Suddenly the door was shoved open and Rakesh stalked into the room.

"I'm sorry, Miss Sharma," Deepak cried, wringing his hands. "He forced his way inside. Shall I ring security?"

Tanvi stood on shaking legs. What on earth was Rakesh doing here? And how did he know where she was? She made a quick decision to hear what he had to say then try to get him out of the suite as quickly as possible. She wanted to avoid causing a scene and she didn't want Alex coming back and finding him there, which could be disastrous. And quite frankly, she was curious about his motives.

"It's okay, Deepak," she said quietly. "I'll be fine."

The valet didn't look convinced, but he left them alone.

Rakesh wandered to the window and stared out, his hands in the pockets of his suit pants.

"What are you doing here, Rakesh?"

He turned and narrowed his eyes on her. "I should be asking you that question," he snarled. "What are you doing in the hotel suite of another man, Tanvi?" He laughed coldly. "I think it's obvious that you're fucking him."

Tanvi gasped and took a step back. "That's none of your business," she murmured.

"Really?" He raised his eyebrows. "And how do you figure that, when you're going to be my wife?"

She inhaled sharply. Was he really going to go there? He was all too aware that she hadn't agreed to anything of the sort.

As if he read her mind, he continued, "I know that you haven't assented, but your consent is inconsequential once your dithering father finally realizes that he needs to make the decision for you, and I believe that day is drawing closer. I happen to know that he grows tired of your unwillingness to conform."

"Why do you want me?" she asked in desperation. "Particularly when you think I've been with another man."

He smiled coldly. "You're beautiful." His lascivious gaze traveled insolently over her. "Your body is exquisite and you come from a good family *and* your dowry is acceptable." He shrugged. "You'll look very good on my arm. But now that you're damaged goods, perhaps the dowry will have to be revised, if I'm to take you off your father's hands."

Tanvi glared at him. "How dare you." She narrowed her eyes on him. "How did you know I was here?"

He chuckled. "Money talks. I just needed to find the right person willing to tell me what I wanted to know." His gaze traveled over her body. "You're looking quite well, by the way. I heard you had an allergy attack."

Tanvi gasped. "What do you know about that?"

"Nothing. Only what Riya told Ajay this morning."

She'd forgotten that Riya's brother was friendly with Rakesh. "I'm fine now, as you can see."

He stepped toward her and it took all of her inner strength to stand her ground. He brushed the back of his hand over her cheek, the touch so soft she could hardly believe that Rakesh was on the other end of it. His eyes glinted angrily and his gentle touch turned hard and rough when he suddenly grabbed her jaw. "I'm looking forward to claiming you as mine," he grated between clenched teeth. "Perhaps this man whose suite you're staying in has broken you in for me. It is such a bore to deal with inexperienced little virgins."

Tanvi swung her hand up to slap him, but he was too quick for her, catching her wrist before she made contact.

"Such a little spitfire," he murmured. "I think I like this fiery side of you. So much more interesting than the serious introvert you were just a short time ago." He squeezed her wrist hard and kept her jaw grasped in his other hand. "Perhaps I have this rich Australian to thank for that. I've heard that the man is particularly handsome." His eyes flashed jealously. "Riya was only too happy to sing his praises the last time I saw her."

Tanvi's heart galloped as she tried to portray an inner strength she didn't feel. Rakesh was starting to scare her and she suddenly wished desperately for Alex to walk through the door. Why had she told Deepak that they didn't need security? She took a deep breath and told herself that Rakesh was just a bully, full of hot wind and nothing else. He wouldn't hurt her. He didn't have it in him, she decided just before he tightened his hold on her jaw and dropped his head to hers.

Chapter Thirty-Two

Alex had managed to make the meeting he expected to miss and, on the way back to the hotel, he'd asked Sanjay about anyone making inquiries about his movements. The driver had been worried that he'd done something wrong and it had taken Alex some time to reassure him that everything was okay. Sanjay eventually remembered that he'd been talking to a driver he hadn't seen before who was driving a tourist couple traveling around India. He'd asked Sanjay about where Alex was going under the guise of wanting to get some ideas for the couple he was driving for. Alex didn't buy it. He also knew that drivers chatted together about anything and everything and Sanjay would have expected that he was helping out a fellow counterpart. Unfortunately, it didn't bring Alex any closer to finding out who was behind the attacks, but he hadn't expected it to be that easy.

He sighed heavily, rubbed his jaw and stared unseeingly out the window, lost in thought. The vibration of his phone snapped him back into the present and he answered on the second ring. "Banks," he snapped into the phone. A very agitated Deepak was on the other end and it took Alex a moment to decipher what he was talking about. When his reason for calling finally sank in, Alex's blood ran cold.

"I'm on my way," he snarled to the valet. "I'll be right there."

He threw his phone across the seat. "Fuck!"

"Is everything all right, boss?" Sanjay asked, his voice full of concern.

"No, it's not. I need to get back to the hotel as quickly as possible."

"Very quick, boss," Sanjay cried. "In two minutes."

True to his word, Sanjay was screeching to a stop outside the hotel in no time at all. Alex jumped from the car and sprinted into the lobby, heading straight for the elevators. His heart was in his throat and adrenaline was coursing through his system for the second time that day.

He reached his floor and stepped from the lift. Taking a deep breath to compose himself, he slid his swipe card into the door lock and walked into the suite.

Deepak met him, hands flapping in agitation. "I'm so sorry, sir," he whispered. "He forced his way in."

Alex waved the valet away and stalked to the living area. What he saw next sent rage surging through his veins. Rakesh had hold of Tanvi's jaw and was kissing her roughly. Tanvi was struggling in his grasp, but obviously no match for the man's strength.

Alex growled low in his throat, two long strides bringing him within striking range. He grabbed the back of the other man's collar and wrenched him aside. Rakesh swung around, fists raised. "What the fuck?"

Alex stepped back and widened his stance, readying himself for a possible attack from Rakesh. Alex assessed the other man and figured that he had at least four inches and thirty pounds on him. If he wanted a fight, Alex would be more than happy to give it to him.

"What the fuck, indeed," Alex snarled. "I walk in here and find you assaulting my girlfriend. You have ten seconds to start running."

Rakesh glowered, his eyes shooting sparks of fury. "Your girlfriend? I don't think so. Hasn't she told you that we're to be married? You are fucking what's mine, not the other way around."

A red haze colored Alex's vision and he grabbed the other man around the throat, squeezing hard. "She is not *yours*, asshole," he grated. "What sort of Neanderthal mentality do you have? There'll be no knocking her on the head with a club and dragging her into your cave, fuckwit."

Rakesh's face began turning a gratifying shade of red, but the man wasn't giving up. For such a lean guy, his neck muscles were surprisingly strong and he was fighting Alex's hold valiantly.

Tanvi raced over to them and grabbed Alex's arm. "Alex, stop. You'll kill him!"

"Does that bother you, my love?" he murmured, his voice low and harsh from his exertion. Tanvi's obvious distress was pissing him off and he dearly wanted to kill the bastard, but he wasn't worth the trouble it would cause him. Finally, he loosened his hold on Rakesh's throat and the man doubled over, wheezing and sputtering. Alex stalked to the door and threw it open. "If I so much as see you look in Tanvi's direction, next time I won't leave you standing," he barked.

Rakesh straightened. "This is not over," he rasped and poked his finger into Alex's chest. "I'll make sure of it."

Tanvi glared at Alex, the sound of the slamming door as Rakesh left still ringing in her ears. "You could have seriously hurt him," she cried.

Alex narrowed his eyes and stormed toward her. "You seem to take a great interest in that man's welfare. Is there more to your relationship than you led me to believe, baby?"

Tanvi fisted her hands on her hips. "No! I just don't want you getting into trouble over him."

Alex reached her and urged her back against the wall, caging her with his body and rubbing a thumb harshly over her lips. "He kissed this mouth," he said, his voice rough. "I need to wash him off you. Did he touch you anywhere else?"

"No," she whispered.

He assessed her for a moment, still rubbing her lips. "Let's shower."

"Yes, good idea," Tanvi agreed. She wanted to get his mind off Rakesh and what he'd said. She was still reeling over his kiss and his totally possessive attitude. *Where did that come from?*

Tanvi followed Alex into the bathroom and stood by as he arranged products on the shelf and turned the water on. He stepped over to her and spun her around so her back was to him. He grasped her hair and twisted it into a knot on top of her head, securing it with one of the large clips she used. He turned her back to him and unbuttoned her blouse and pushed it off her shoulders. He wrapped his arms around her waist and unzipped her skirt, tugging it past her hips and down her legs until she could step out of it, leaving her standing in her lace bra and panties.

"I don't have any other clothes with me," she pointed out as he started to undress.

"I rang Riya and asked her to pack a bag for you and leave it at reception. She left her phone number with the staff. She wanted me to call her and let her know how you were. I'll have Deepak check to see if she's delivered it yet."

He picked up the bathroom phone and spoke to Deepak as Tanvi let her gaze travel over his firm body. Clad only in tight black boxers, he looked the epitome of everything alpha male. His physique truly was extraordinary. She shimmied out of her bra and panties and stepped into the shower recess. Alex removed his boxers a moment later and joined her under the warm spray. He picked up the shower gel, squirted some onto a bath sponge and started smoothing it over her skin, starting at her shoulders and clavicle and caressing in circles around her breasts and down her torso to her tummy. He knelt on the floor and soaped between her thighs then down each of her legs.

"Turn around," he instructed, his voice rough.

She did as he asked and he washed her back and ass, caressing the sponge between her butt cheeks for long delicious moments, sparking a low moan from deep in her throat.

He spun her around to face him and urged her back against the cool tiles. Picking up a tube of cleanser, he then squirted some into his palm. "Close your eyes."

She closed them and he rubbed his soaped hands over her face, paying particular attention to her mouth. She smiled inwardly at his insistence in ridding any signs of Rakesh from her body and she was happy to accommodate him. He rinsed the cleanser off her face with a cloth, gently rubbing it around her eyes and over her lips.

"You're clean now," he murmured in her ear. "Now I'm going to replace his touch with mine."

She tipped her head back just as his lips touched hers and he took her in a deep, passionate kiss. She moaned into his mouth and snaked her tongue out to dance with his. She threw her hands around his neck and melted against him as he kissed her fiercely and hungrily. He skimmed his hands down her sides and cupped her ass, tugging her tightly to his body so she could feel his erection, throbbing and hot, against her belly.

"Please," she whispered.

He nibbled on her bottom lip, then he licked her where his teeth had been before plunging his tongue into her mouth once more and slanting his lips across hers. Warmth bloomed in her core and radiated outward. When they were like this, together in each other's arms, so intimately connected, nothing else mattered.

Alex tightened his grip on her ass and lifted her, using the shower wall to support her back. "Wrap those legs around me, baby," he rasped in her ear.

She did as he asked and he plunged into her in one deep thrust. She gulped as he stretched her, filling her completely.

"Fuck, you're so hot and slick." He grunted and stilled inside her, his heaving breaths signaling his effort to maintain control.

Tanvi wrapped her arms around his neck, digging her nails into his shoulder blades. He hissed and gripped her ass cheeks, bouncing her hard on his solid cock. She moaned and threw her head back against the tiles, relishing the feel of Alex taking her so completely. He skimmed his lips across her jaw and down her throat, licking and kissing her flesh and sending shooting sparks of pleasure straight to her nipples. She cried out and tightened her legs around his waist, arching her back. He growled, dropped his head and latched on to her nipple, biting the tight nub until tears pricked her eyes. She whimpered and writhed and pushed her hips down to take more of him inside her. He pumped up, yanking her down simultaneously to meet his thrusts. She felt the stirring deep in her belly, the sensations building and swelling.

He pulled all the way out, his biceps cording deliciously under her hands as he grasped her ass and took all her weight. As he lunged back in slowly and deliberately, his cock barbell dragged over her folds, sending shivers of delight rippling down her spine.

"I'm close," she whispered.

"I know," he said, his voice tight with need. "Not yet!"

He thrust again, using his brute strength to maneuver her to his liking, pumping in long languid strokes and using his cock piercing to hit her in just the right places.

"Please, Alex," she begged, so close that her insides were throbbing and aching for release. She held on to his shoulders, incapable of any movement, as Alex had taken total control, pushing and pulling her onto his steel-hard erection and circling his hips when he bottomed out in her.

"I can't take any more. I'm coming!" Pleasure scorched through her, tightening her insides and sparking ferocious spasms in her core.

"That's it!" Alex barked then latched on to her neck, sucking hard as he thrust up and pumped her full of his cum.

Chapter Thirty-Three

Alex picked up the bag Deepak had collected and took it into the bedroom. Tanvi was sitting on the bed in the hotel cotton robe, brushing her hair. He leaned on the doorjamb and watched her. He could watch her brush her hair all night. There was something sensual yet innocent about the act. The soft light from the side lamp shone delicately on her and highlighted her lush breasts under the filmy cotton robe. Fuck, he was getting hard again. He didn't think another woman had ever managed to affect his libido so much.

He cleared his throat, wandered into the room and placed the bag at her feet. "Riya collected these from your house."

Tanvi looked up at him. "I wonder what my parents thought of her rummaging through my things?"

"She told them that you're staying at her house and you had a late meeting so she volunteered to pick them up for you. Does it matter?"

She bit her bottom lip. "I guess not. I had this conversation with my father the other day, actually." She shrugged. "It just became a habit after a while to tell them my plans. I put a stop to it last night and I'm no longer informing them of all my movements."

Alex raised his eyebrows. "I'm glad, otherwise they might require bypass surgery or some defibrillator action."

She giggled and slapped him on the arm with her brush.

He smirked. "Get dressed."

"Are we going somewhere?"

Alex looked down at his black pajama bottoms. "I thought we'd eat here. I think we have some things to discuss. But I'd prefer that Deepak not see you looking so delectable in that hotel gown."

She frowned. "I hardly think this gown constitutes as sexy."

He dropped a kiss to her head. "I disagree, particularly when the light hits you just right."

Her gasps of feigned outrage followed him out of the bedroom and he chuckled. He loved it when he made her blush.

He met Deepak in the kitchen and requested a simple dinner of grilled chicken, rice and vegetables. He'd have loved some seafood. However, he never ordered it in New Delhi. He knew that the hotel would have only the freshest ingredients, but it was a thing of his never to order seafood unless he was close to the sea. Perhaps he and Tanvi could take a trip to the south of India — the seafood curries there were delicious.

He selected something soft on his iPod. He wanted unobtrusive background music. A movement in the doorway caught his attention and he looked up. Tanvi was standing just inside the entrance of the dining area, staring at him. Even dressed in yoga pants and a silk blouse she was stunning. She licked her lips, her gaze traveling up and down his body.

He raised his eyebrows. "And what has you so enthralled?"

She smiled. "I was just admiring your body. It's so" — she waved a hand in the air — "muscular."

He chuckled. "I'm glad you like what you see." He allowed his gaze to drift over her. "I was admiring you too. Those tight yoga pants that hug your ass and that soft blouse is giving me just a hint of the deliciousness that hides underneath." He stepped toward her, drew her into his arms and dropped his head to nuzzle her neck. "You look hot in anything you wear." He nipped her throat then licked where his teeth had been. "But I prefer you in nothing."

She gasped and dropped her head back, giving him better access to her neck. He took full advantage and locked his mouth on her flesh, sucking and nibbling. Then, grabbing her ass, her pulled her tight to his pelvis and ground his erection against her.

"You're going to mark me again if you're not careful," she said huskily. "It took me forever to cover the last one."

He growled against her throat. "I like to see my mark on you."

It wasn't lost on him that he was acting in a similar way to Rakesh. This need he had to claim Tanvi, to show the world that she belonged to him, wasn't that far removed from Rakesh's cave-man attitude. He pulled back and gazed at her neck, at the red stain blooming under her smooth caramel-colored flesh. He rubbed the bruise with his thumb. "I've marked you again. I'm sorry," he murmured.

She straightened and looked up at him. "I like it," she whispered, cupping his jaw in her hand and caressing his bottom lip with her thumb.

He tightened his hold on her ass and gazed down. "You don't think it's some possessive macho bullshit?"

She giggled, the sound like music to his ears.

"Perhaps," she conceded. "But I like that it's coming from you."

"Is that why you wore your hair down today, to cover my mark? I saw you in the restaurant this morning, before your allergy attack. I wondered why your hair wasn't in the usual braid you wear for work."

She smiled up at him. "It was one of the reasons. The other was that I had a need to feel feminine." She blushed. "And just a little sexy."

He narrowed his eyes, his jaw tensing in anger. "I didn't like it." He squeezed her ass cheeks to make his point. "Men were looking at you," he continued, his voice low. "I want to be the only man looking at you and you shouldn't want any other bastard's eyes shooting your way. Why did you want to look sexy, particularly when we hadn't planned to see each other today?"

He kept his voice low, but he was sure she could detect the undercurrent of anger. He closed his eyes and breathed deeply. It wasn't Tanvi's fault that he couldn't tolerate the thought of other men looking at her. He recalled the resentment he'd felt that morning when he'd seen her in the restaurant and wanted to kick himself for his possessiveness. Problem was, he couldn't seem to help himself when it came to her. He opened his eyes and gazed down into her worried ones.

She bit her bottom lip. "I'm not sure."

It took him a moment to realize that she was answering his last question.

"I think because I felt so bad about what happened last night. How it was unfair of me to lash out at you and I needed to feel better about myself." She shrugged. "I guess you could say that I wanted some feminine armor."

A thrill rippled down Tanvi's spine—she had to admit that Alex's anger and possessiveness were a real turn-on.

When a vicious asshole like Rakesh tried to dominate her, she was appalled and when he touched her, her skin crawled, but what she felt for Alex was three hundred sixty degrees in the opposite direction. When Alex dominated her, she felt almost powerful. It was as if she was the one in control and he'd told her often enough that she, in fact, did hold the power.

Alex smiled at her. "Well, I want your hair to be mine. I want you to wear it down only for me." He nuzzled her neck again, sending bolts of sensation to her nipples. "You look gorgeous," he mumbled against her flesh, "with those beautiful tresses tumbling down your back. Like sex and woman and like you've just been fucked, hard."

She shivered and dropped her head back, relishing in the feel of him nuzzling and nipping her throat.

"You must know that when other men see you like that, that's what they envision—you, in bed, after sex. That image is only for me."

He was hot and hard and throbbing insistently against her belly. She wriggled in his embrace, warmth blooming in her core and firing sparks of pleasure outward.

"Is. That. Unreasonable?" he asked between licks and nibbles. "That I want that only for me?"

"No," she gasped as the blooming warmth turned to a boiling inferno. "I want you to have it."

All thought left her and she melted against him, her legs turning to jelly so that Alex had to take her weight. He cupped her ass with one hand, pulling her up his body and twisting his other fist in her hair. She wondered vaguely at his strength to be able to lift her so easily. His mouth was now level with hers. "You're so strong," she murmured against his lips. "It's hot."

He twisted his fist tighter in her hair and pulled her head back so she was once more looking up at him. He dipped his head and kissed her deeply, snaking his tongue into her mouth and winding it with hers. She tasted coffee and cinnamon and she deepened their kiss, wanting more of him. She moaned into his mouth, wrapped her legs around his waist and pressed her pelvis down to feel his cock between her thighs, her yoga tights and the satin of his pajama pants hardly a barrier to the sensation.

He growled and cupped her ass tighter, pushing her down onto his straining erection. His cock kicked, punching her between her thighs and sparking a groan from deep in her throat. *How can this keep getting better and how will I live without it?* Alex's hunger for her was animalistic and primal, his arousal so powerful that she was heady with it. He was twisting her hair tighter, his fist so close to her scalp that tears pricked her eyes. She welcomed the pain, rejoiced in it. It told her that she was alive, alive with these wonderful sensations and emotions — that she was *living*.

"Please," she begged into his mouth, grinding herself down on his length, uncaring that he was holding her up using just one arm and his thighs. He wouldn't drop her, she knew that with a certainty and she trusted him implicitly.

Chapter Thirty-Four

Alex was crazed with his arousal. He couldn't believe that he'd taken Tanvi just half an hour ago in the shower. He felt as if he hadn't fucked her in months. He deepened their kiss, scoring her lips roughly with his own and gripping her hair hard. He could feel her moisture through their clothes. Her pussy was so juicy with her desire that he could smell it. Her scent was tingeing the air and heightening his own rabid need.

He groaned into her mouth and swung them around, to walk toward the bank of windows. He'd opened one earlier to let some air in, the room being so high that the smog and noise of the Delhi traffic didn't reach them.

He placed Tanvi on her feet, grasped the waist of her tights and pulled them down. She stepped out of them and kicked them aside. He groaned when he realized she wasn't wearing panties and he plunged two fingers into her pussy. She was hot and tight and so wet. "Oh, baby," he breathed. "You're so ready for me."

He spun her around so she was facing the open window, only the waist-high rails separating them from a twenty-story drop. "Grip the rail," he demanded in her ear.

She stiffened and tried to step back but his body prevented her from going anywhere. "Are you afraid of heights, baby?"

She shook her head. "We're just so high," she whispered.

Alex urged her back toward the window. He placed his arms at either side of her body and gripped the rail, caging her in. "Do you trust me?"

She nodded, but remained rigid against him.

"Do you know that I won't hurt you? That I'd do anything to keep you safe?"

She nodded again.

"I want an answer," he demanded.

"Yes, sir."

"Good girl. Now relax against me." He released one hand from his grip on the rail and skimmed it down her torso, stopping at her pussy and sifting his fingers through her wet folds. "That's it, sweetness," he coaxed, as she melted into him and moaned. "Now. Grip. The. Rail."

She did as he asked, grasping so tightly her knuckles turned white.

He pushed his pajama pants down and anchored the waistband under his balls. "I won't let you fall," he murmured. "Don't let go of the rail."

This was a small test to ensure that he had her complete trust. He'd never force her to do something she didn't want to do, but he wanted her to submit to him, to have total conviction that he'd keep her safe.

He grasped her hips, bent his knees and skimmed his aching cock between her folds, spreading her moisture and hitting her clit with his barbell.

She trembled and pushed her ass back into him. He swept her blouse up, tucking it under the strap of her bra to keep it in place. Then he grasped her hips again, straightened his legs and entered her in one hard thrust.

She gasped and threw her head back. "Argh!"

He pulled out and thrust again. He kept his strokes steady and slow and the strain was killing him. She felt so good, wet and hot and compact—like a fist around his cock.

Alex closed his eyes for a moment, stilled and took a deep breath. "Are you okay?" he asked, his voice rough.

"Yes! Move, please move!"

He squeezed her hips, a silent warning to watch what she said. He groaned, pulled all the way out and thrust home, seating himself balls deep. He started a steady rhythm, pumping his hips with sure, languid strokes and gripping her waist to move her in time with his thrusts.

She moaned and writhed and gave herself over to him completely. He watched her hands closely, ensuring that she kept a tight hold of the rail as she started to lose her control. If she let go, she could hit her head on the bar and he wouldn't allow that to happen.

He could feel the telltale fluttering and quivering in her core, signaling that she was drawing near to release. He swept his hands up her torso, yanked her bra cups down and pinched each of her nipples. She cried out, stiffened then came hard, trembling and shaking, her inner muscles clamping around his erection and milking him.

He glanced down. Tanvi's feet were dangling off the ground and it hit him, like a lightning bolt to his gut, that the only thing holding her up at that moment was his cock inside her, her grip on the rail merely a safety mechanism. That was it. The knowledge that he was holding her up by his dick sent him hurtling over the abyss.

"Fuck!" He squeezed her breasts, lunged hard and roared as he filled her full of his cum.

Alex worked to steady his breathing. That last orgasm was one of the most intense he'd ever experienced and his heart was bashing against his rib cage like a jackhammer.

"I can't feel my legs," Tanvi murmured after a moment.

"That's because your legs aren't holding you up," he muttered, releasing his hold on her breasts and dragging his hands down to her hips.

She twisted her head around. "What do you mean?"

He looked down pointedly and she followed his gaze, her eyes widening.

"Yes," he smirked. "My cock's holding you up and I'm still rock-hard." He bent his head forward and brushed a kiss over her lips. "It's so fucking erotic that I want to stay like this forever."

She giggled. "And my hands on the rail," she pointed out.

"No, sweetness. If you let go, you'd fall face first but your legs would still be dangling a foot off the floor. Your hands on the rail are merely for balance and safety."

He straightened, steadied her with his hands on her hips, bent his knees and lowered her to the floor while he pulled out. He mourned the loss of her snug warmth around his cock, but unfortunately he couldn't stay like that forever, as much as he wanted to. He readjusted his pajama pants, pulling them up so they once more sat low on his hips.

"Fuck," he muttered, pushing a hand through his hair. "I'm in danger of fucking you into a coma."

She giggled again and he loved the sound. He smiled and pulled her blouse back down. "Get dressed, baby. Deepak will be in soon with dinner."

Tanvi scurried into the bathroom, washed up and dragged on a pair of loose cotton pants. She assessed herself in the mirror, her eyes were bright and her cheeks flushed, her hair a tumbling mass around her shoulders. Yes, she looked like she'd just had an energetic session of lovemaking. She decided not to brush the tangles out of her hair, as it would distract Alex. The thought made her smile.

When she emerged in the dining room, Deepak was setting their dinner on the table while Alex was pouring wine.

He looked up. "Sit." He indicated the place opposite him. "I ordered a light meal. I thought that, after this morning, we should try for something basic. I've had Deepak prepare it and I'd prefer you don't eat anywhere else until we have this" — he waved a hand in the air — "whatever *it* is, sorted out."

She smiled her thanks and took a seat. Alex was right. It would be prudent to be careful. She'd come to the stark realization that afternoon that her allergy attack couldn't have been an accident. She'd been eating those pastries for a long time and she knew that food labeled appropriate for allergy sufferers was always meticulously prepared. Anything less was too risky, so the only other explanation was that someone had tampered with her food.

She took a bite of chicken. It was lightly sprinkled with a fragrant masala and tasted delicious and moist.

"I spoke to Jay this morning," Alex said. "He's going to make some discreet inquiries. I'm not sure if anything will come of it but you never know. People talk and even something said in passing might take us closer to discovering who's behind these attacks. Also, I don't think the suspect pool is particularly large."

"No," she agreed. "But I still can't see what Rakesh would get out of it. I've told you, he's never seemed remotely interested in me."

Alex gave her a pointed look. "He seemed very put out this afternoon. In fact, he appeared downright possessive. Not the actions of an indifferent man, I would suggest."

She frowned. "It *was* odd behavior from him. Perhaps he feels that you in my life is threatening his chance at my dowry."

"And he fucking *should* feel threatened," Alex snapped. "As far as I'm concerned, that marriage is no more taking place than me taking a trip to the moon tomorrow."

He picked up his knife and fork and continued to eat. Tanvi got the message he was sending—subject closed. She sighed and took a sip of her wine. Unfortunately, Alex's opinion on the matter wasn't the only one that counted, and she miserably suspected that this time was one instance when Alex wouldn't get what he wanted.

Chapter Thirty-Five

Alex had just arrived back at the hotel to have a late lunch with Jay. His friend had called him earlier to say that he had news regarding who was behind the attacks on Tanvi and ever since, Alex had been sitting through meetings trying unsuccessfully to concentrate. Finally, he'd been in a position to leave the rest of the discussions to his team and he'd quickly departed.

He met Jay in his office where a cold lunch had been set out for them on the small conference table.

"I thought we'd have more privacy in here," Jay explained.

Alex smiled his thanks and took a seat opposite him. "You have some news?" he asked immediately.

"I do. I'm pretty sure I know who's behind these threats, or, more specifically, attacks."

"Yes?"

"I think it's Rakesh."

Alex put down his knife and fork. "I knew it! He forced his way into my suite yesterday when I wasn't there and confronted Tanvi."

"What?" Jay asked sharply. "How did he know your suite number and how did he get onto the guest floors? Our security prohibits just anyone from wandering around."

"Apparently he paid a staff member."

Jay shoved a hand through his hair. "Shit. It's a constant problem we have to face. Offer enough money here and you can get almost anything done. We vet our staff as best we can, but people always have family members to take care of, financial or medical problems... The list goes on. There's generally someone who can be manipulated with the offer of money."

Alex waved away Jay's apologies. "It can happen anywhere, my friend. Money talks all over the world. What did you discover?"

"Rakesh has been largely indifferent to marrying Tanvi. By all accounts, the man is ruthless and conceited. His main goal is to make money, as much of it as possible and his ethics in doing so are questionable. But the other thing to remember is that here in India, loss of face is a big deal, as is one's honor."

Alex nodded. "I understand. Go on."

"Apparently a group of Rakesh's important business associates saw him with Tanvi one evening and they were most impressed. They commented on her beauty and sophistication and how she'd make a lucky man a good wife. Rakesh, of course, told them all that he was going to marry her, that the arrangements were nearing completion. It's also a topic of discussion between his friends. There's...been some jealousy, rivalry, if you will. Tanvi's considered an excellent catch, Alex, and

Rakesh has been telling anyone who will listen that she's his, or soon will be. Now that you've come on the scene and disrupted everything, he's terrified of losing face and of having his honor disrespected and he'll do anything to avoid that."

Alex sat back in his chair. "Even if it means killing her?" he asked incredulously.

Jay shrugged. "I'm sure he doesn't love her. He'd consider it a small sacrifice to save his honor and keep his reputation among those most important to him. If she were dead, of course, the problem would go away. Or even if she was sick or maimed, it would be acceptable, expected almost, that he wouldn't marry her."

"I think Tanvi suspects it's her uncle," Alex murmured.

"That man also has questionable ethics," Jay responded. "But I don't believe he knows anything about the attacks on Tanvi." Jay gave him a pointed look. "Her saving grace at the moment is the fact that you've kept your relationship discreet. If you were seen blatantly in public together, the outcome could have been a lot worse. I suspect that Rakesh has been keeping tabs on Tanvi, for reasons only he could divulge, and that's how he came to know of her association with you."

Fuck. Alex tugged on his hair. No wonder Tanvi was concerned about public outings. He was aware that honor killings still occurred, but the idea appalled him. He just couldn't wrap his Western thinking around such a concept. "Wouldn't it be a great risk?" he asked. "For Rakesh to kill her? What if he was caught?"

"The court system works very slowly here and Rakesh has connections in high places. Plus, he's been careful to pose the attacks as accidents and it would be difficult to prove otherwise."

Alex dropped his head into his hands and rubbed his temples. It was worse than he thought. He suddenly realized what Tanvi had been trying to tell him all along, that the situation was indeed complicated and perhaps there was no easy fix. When family honor was involved, it seemed that anything was acceptable in order to protect it. He felt impotent and with it a burning rage engulfed him. He was unused to the emotion. He was accustomed to getting what he wanted, or working toward a satisfactory outcome. This situation was so alien and confusing that it left him feeling helpless.

He lifted his head. "Do you have any advice?"

Jay rubbed his chin thoughtfully. "It's my understanding that the marriage arrangement is not yet official. Is that correct?"

"As far as I know. Tanvi told me that her father is losing patience with her refusal to agree. Apparently he's given her time to come to terms with it, but recently he told her that he was going to make the decision for her."

"Okaay," Jay said slowly. "That tells me that the arrangement is not yet official. Regardless of what Rakesh has been saying to his acquaintances, his family might not have the same expectations. Rakesh has been trying to deal with the problem of Tanvi's reluctance quietly. I dare say he had no concerns about the marriage going ahead until you came along. He would have been confident that Tanvi's family would have eventually forced her into it. Now he feels threatened. Even I can see the changes in her and I don't know her particularly well. She's more confident, more forthright

and Rakesh can see her slipping through his fingers."
Jay sat forward and gave Alex an intense look. "Think
carefully about what I next ask you."

Alex nodded, a strong feeling of anxiety coiling in his
gut.

"What are your feelings for Tanvi? How serious are
you about her? I ask this because if you're working
toward her *not* marrying Rakesh, she'll need you to
support her and protect her, in more ways than one.
Her family won't agree to her not marrying him, just to
spare your feelings or hers. They obviously believe that
Rakesh will make a good and appropriate match. The
only way that Tanvi can avoid it is if another,
equivalent, or more suitable match is made."

Alex's mind was reeling. *What the fuck is Jay
suggesting?*

"Her options are limited," Jay continued. "She could
run away, of course. You could take her back to
Australia, but visas take time to organize and that's
only temporary and you know as well as I that
residency visas for Australia can take years to approve.
While that was being arranged, she'd need somewhere
to live in between her visits to Australia. She could start
fresh somewhere else in India, but with no family or
friends to assist her, the chances of her doing that
successfully are slim."

Alex frowned, lost deep in thought. Tanvi was right.
Jay had pretty much just confirmed that if Tanvi
refused to marry in accordance with her family's
wishes, there was a very real probability that they
would cut her off, and where would she be then? She
worked at her father's firm, lived in their home.

Fuck! He couldn't stand the thought of Tanvi
marrying Rakesh, but her family was backing her into

a corner. He felt a rage unlike he'd ever felt at the thought of *Rakesh*, of *anyone*, touching her — being with her. He clenched his hands into fists, his jaw tightening with tension.

"She can't marry that bastard," Alex eventually ground out. "Is there any way to stop this?"

Jay sat back. "I know Tanvi's father, as you're aware, and his firm is contracted to us to provide financial services. He's a good man, if somewhat misguided. I don't think he'd want his only child marrying a man who tried to kill her." He shrugged. "But perhaps there's something he wants from Rakesh I don't know. I had heard that the Sharma company was experiencing financial difficulties but I'm not sure how true that is." Jay gave Alex a level look. "The only course of action I can suggest is to go to her home, talk to her father and tell him that you want to marry Tanvi."

Silence filled the room as Alex digested what his friend had just said. He expected to experience panic, heart palpitations or at the very least incredulity at Jay's suggestion but an odd tranquility had descended on him. His subconscious, he realized, had been pointing him in this direction and, oddly, he felt no concern, no fear about the prospect. It was because he loved her. Slowly but surely, he'd been falling for her. Tanvi had insinuated herself into his very being, had wrapped herself around his psyche like an addictive drug. He couldn't allow anything to happen to her. He had to protect her at all costs.

"I'll go tomorrow. What's the best way to approach this?"

"I'll go with you. You'll stand a much better chance with me vouching for you and I can also verify the attempts that Rakesh has made on Tanvi's life. I'll call Mr. Sharma and tell him that I need to see him."

"What about our different religions? Will that be a problem?"

Jay shrugged. "I don't know what Mr. Sharma sees as a priority. Of course, the fact that you are successful and wealthy will prove highly in your favor. Every parent wants a good match for their child. One of the reasons is that they also want security. Parents want to feel confident that they'll be taken care of in their older age. India is not a country where retirement homes or aged care facilities are popular. The accepted norm here is that children take care of their elderly." He took a deep breath and let it out slowly. "Alex, he can still refuse you. This is by no means a done deal."

Alex nodded. "I'm aware. I've been designing a contingency plan while you've been talking." He paused for a moment. "If his business *is* suffering, perhaps I can use it to my advantage. I have something that most people find attractive — money. Of course, all this rests on the fact that Tanvi actually *wants* to marry me. I haven't even asked her yet."

Jay chuckled. "Yes, we're getting a little ahead of ourselves, but, from what I've seen, I think her feelings are very much like yours."

Chapter Thirty-Six

Tanvi sighed as she hung up the phone. She'd just explained to her mother that she would be staying at Riya's house for the next few days and she didn't even feel guilty for lying. Why should she when the whole reason she was stuck as a virtual prisoner in the hotel was because of the madman her parents wanted her to marry?

She thought back to her earlier conversation with Alex, when he'd explained that Rakesh had been behind the attacks and why. She was still having a hard time fully comprehending it, but the more she considered the situation, the more it started to make sense. Rakesh was the type of man who would stop at nothing to maintain his credibility and to avoid loss of face. Alex had described how Rakesh had been effectively using her to gain esteem and respect within his business circles, and his friends, apparently. She'd scoffed at that, but then Alex had scolded her and shown her in no uncertain terms just how beautiful and sexy he thought she was. It made sense to her now how Rakesh could become so furious after discovering that she'd been involved in a sexual relationship with Alex. He hadn't cared that he wouldn't be marrying a virgin, and Tanvi wasn't about to enlighten him that it wasn't Alex who had popped that cherry. He'd seemed to relish the idea of having a woman broken in for him, as he'd so crassly termed it. No, it appeared solely to be the fact that her relationship with Alex, such as it was, presented an unreasonable risk to his reputation. As Alex had succinctly put it—Rakesh wanted her for arm candy, to impress his business associates and his friends. He wanted to be the guy the others envied.

She stared despondently at the clothes that Riya had packed for her, a heavy depression settling over her, thick and dark. Alex had said he had a surprise for her that evening and that she should dress for dinner, but she wasn't excited by the prospect. She knew this relationship they had would soon come to an end. It had to—what other options were there? Rakesh was obviously not giving her up. A part of her had hoped that when he discovered that she wasn't pure, that he wouldn't be her first, he'd be disgusted and he wouldn't want her. Instead, he'd surprised the life out of her by seeming almost pleased with the fact. She couldn't wrap her head around him. Just when she thought she had him figured out, he did something to surprise her.

She selected a dress in black crepe. It was low cut and hugged her figure. She'd never worn it before and she knew why Riya had packed it—it would appeal to the sauciness in Riya's nature. Tanvi had bought it on a whim, but had always been too scared to wear it, knowing her father probably wouldn't have let her out of the house in it. She selected lingerie in black lace, the bra a demi so it would work perfectly. She slid into the underwear and stepped into her dress, zipping it up the side. She was glad that Riya had packed her gold heels. They were strappy and very high and would put her at a height more conducive to Alex's six-foot-three frame. She applied a light cover of foundation and dusted her face with powder. Her eyes, she knew, were one of her best features. She highlighted the hazel-green orbs in black liner, coated the lids in silver-gray and brushed her lashes in thick black mascara. She glossed her lips in a pale pink and gazed at her reflection critically. A smoky-eyed vixen stared back at her. She was happy with the results and knew instinctively that Alex would be too. She debated about her hair — Alex liked it down, but only for him — she recalled his jealous outburst of earlier. She shrugged, and brushed it until it hung in a shiny veil down her back, then, on impulse, she flipped her head upside down and sprayed hairspray to the underside, scrunching her hair at the same time. Her messy tresses were exactly the look she was going for. It would drive Alex wild.

The door lock buzzed and, a moment later, Alex strode into the bedroom. He'd been back earlier to shower and change, then he'd left again, not telling her where he was going. She allowed her gaze to travel over his firm body. His gray slacks hung off his lean hips and he'd rolled his dress shirt to the elbows, revealing muscular forearms. The top two buttons of his shirt were undone, giving her a glimpse of his tan chest, speckled with dark-blond hair. He truly was a stunning example of manhood and every time she looked at him her heart stuttered. She had to wonder at her good fortune, a good fortune that she knew would soon end.

Alex stared hard at Tanvi—she looked good enough to eat, which he hoped to do later. He growled low in his throat at the messy mass of hair tumbling around her shoulders. She looked like she'd just gotten out of a man's bed, where she'd been fucked hard. He stepped toward her and lifted a lock, twirling it through his fingers. "Are you trying to drive me insane?" he asked, his voice soft.

She shook her head.

"Because I told you this afternoon that I don't want other men to see this. Already you're defying me."

She looked up at him, her bottom lip trapped between her teeth. "This will be over soon," she whispered. "You'll go back to Australia and I'll continue with my life here. I thought I'd do my hair the way you like it, one last time."

He frowned and clenched his jaw in anger. "Why do you insist on talking like this?"

She gave a little shrug. "I'm just being realistic."

He tamped his anger down and reminded himself that she didn't know what he had arranged. He'd been planning all afternoon, thinking about contingency strategies and the best way to approach her father. He'd also visited the jeweler in the hotel and purchased an engagement ring, a cushion-cut, three-karat solitaire diamond. Perhaps it was overkill but he felt that something excessive would appeal to her family and would also demonstrate his wealth and commitment. Anything less was not an option. Now that he'd made the decision to ask her to marry him, he felt at ease for the first time in days. Of course, his family would be surprised, but they'd accept her unconditionally, because he loved her.

"Are you ready?" he asked.

She nodded and picked up a gold and black clutch.

He held his arm out to her. "Come."

Alex guided Tanvi out of the suite and into the elevator. He pressed the button for the top floor. He'd booked out the entire restaurant for dinner. Jay had organized it for him. Apparently it had taken quite a few calls to people and quite a few promises made to cancel all the reservations.

They arrived at the top floor and Alex ushered Tanvi out of the elevator and toward the restaurant entrance. She stopped at the doorway, a look of puzzlement crossing her features.

"It's just us," he murmured, placing his hand on her lower back and nudging her forward.

"Are you serious?"

"Very. I wanted you all to myself."

She smiled brightly and giggled. "You are very excessive."

He shrugged and smiled back at her. "With you, I guess I am."

The maître d' hurried over to them. "Welcome, Mr. Banks. Everything is ready for you."

Alex thanked the man and they followed him to a table set in the middle of the room. A string quartet played quietly and unobtrusively in the background. A bunch of lilies in a low vase graced the table as a beautiful centerpiece. Candles floated in the water, providing a romantic ambience.

"It's lovely," Tanvi breathed.

Alex pulled her chair out for her and she took her seat, smiling her thanks.

"I've ordered already," Alex murmured. A moment later, a waiter arrived bearing a tray of beautifully made hors d'oeuvres. Bite-sized curry puffs, onion bhajis and little crab cakes were deposited on the table. Another waiter opened a bottle of French champagne, popping the cork with celebratory cheer.

Alex fidgeted, his palms were sweaty and he realized with a jolt that he was nervous. He'd been going to wait until dessert to ask the big question, but he couldn't delay. There was no way he'd be able to sit through dinner making polite conversation and pretending that all was as it should be.

He grasped the ring box in his hand and got up from the table. He bent on one knee in front of Tanvi and took her hand.

She gasped, her other hand flying to her mouth.

"Tanvi Sharma, will you do me the honor of becoming my wife? Will you marry me?"

Chapter Thirty-Seven

Tanvi couldn't believe what she was seeing and hearing and it took a moment for her to catch her breath.

Alex opened the box and she gasped anew at the beautiful diamond he revealed. He quirked an eyebrow expectantly and she realized that he was waiting for her answer.

"Yes," she cried, flinging her arms around his shoulders. "Yes, I'll marry you!"

Tears of joy streamed down her cheeks and she brushed them away with the back of her hand. She knew her mascara and eyeliner would be smeared and she'd look a mess but she didn't care. She could hardly believe what Alex had asked her. He grasped her hand and slid the ring onto her left ring finger. It fit perfectly, the diamond glinting richly in the candlelight.

Alex leaned forward and took her mouth in a lush kiss, slipping his tongue out to stroke and tangle with hers. She moaned into his mouth and flung her arms around his shoulders, her tummy fluttering wildly with butterflies. Languidly, he pulled back, brushing her lips with his again before standing up to retake his seat.

Slowly the potential problems they faced started to creep into her subconscious, taking some of the shine off her happiness. She dabbed at her face and eyes with her napkin. "I'm not sure what my father will say," she mumbled. "What if he says no to you?"

"I've thought about that and I have a plan, but it would mean you having to defy your parents. Let's think positively. Jay is coming with me and we're seeing your father tomorrow. We're going to tell him about Rakesh and I'm going to ask him for permission to marry you."

"Where will we live?"

"I was hoping you'd move to Australia with me. That's where my business is, but we can come back to India once a year for a visit."

Tanvi nodded. She'd always wanted to go to Australia and the prospect of living there appealed to her. In fact, she just wanted to be where Alex was.

"We'll need to arrange visas for you and you might have to leave the country a couple of times until we sort out a residency visa but it should be easier if we're married." He shrugged and smiled. "I pay a lot of lawyers a lot of money, so they should be good for something."

Tanvi was bursting with happiness. She had to have faith that her father would agree. And she trusted Alex. If he had a plan, she would follow it, even if it meant defying her parents. She'd decided that her happiness was the priority and spending the rest of her life with Alex was what she wanted — what she needed.

* * * *

Tanvi had been pacing endlessly around the suite, her nerves settling into her stomach like a lead weight.

Alex and Jay had left over two hours ago to talk to her parents. She couldn't decide if the length of time they were away was a good thing or a bad thing. At least she supposed her parents were listening to them, which was something.

She wrung her hands in agitation, the sun catching her diamond and reflecting rainbow colors on the wall. They'd decided that she would stay at the hotel, and if her parents said no, Alex would take Tanvi back to the house to pack up her things and she would leave with him. She hoped desperately it wouldn't come to that. She loved her parents, but she couldn't go along with their wishes where Rakesh was concerned. She knew that she'd be destined for a bleak existence if she were to marry him and, after Alex, that wasn't an option for her. She looked at her watch again and sighed in exasperation. She didn't think she'd ever felt so anxious.

A noise at the door made her jump and, a moment later, Alex strode through. Tanvi searched his face for some sign of how things had gone, but he was remarkably impassive.

She ran over to him, throwing her arms around his neck. "What happened?" she mumbled against his chest.

Alex gripped her wrists and pulled her arms down by her sides. "Let's sit."

She followed him over to the sofa and settled on the edge, her heart hammering so hard she was surprised it wasn't audible.

"We explained to your parents what Rakesh did, how he endangered your life. They were surprised to say the least, but they did believe us. I'm glad Jay was with me, as your father knows him well and obviously respects him. Also, Jay went as far as to say that if you did marry Rakesh, then he'd have to terminate the Totally Five Star contract with your father's firm. He explained that he wouldn't risk such a close relationship with someone who could have caused irreparable to damage to the hotel's reputation."

Tanvi blinked, eyes wide. That threat certainly would have received her father's undivided attention. He considered the hotel one of his top clients. To risk losing them was something he would not take lightly.

She focused her attention back on Alex.

"I asked your father for your hand in marriage. Your parents were speechless initially and quite suspicious, not knowing anything about me. I explained to them what I could provide you. I also declined a dowry and offered him anything to assist his company and I suggested that I could send quite a lot of business his way. Which I would make a priority if he were to give us his blessing."

Tanvi's nerves were close to snapping point. "What did he say?" she asked desperately.

"He didn't say no. We could consider it a provisional yes."

Did she just hear that correctly? Until that moment, she'd been afraid that it was all too good to be true, that kismet was going to step in and interfere. "I can't believe it," she whispered then frowned. "Provisional yes? What does that mean?"

Alex took her hand. "Your parents know nothing about me, having only met me for the first time today. Understandably they have some concerns."

He grasped her around the waist and lifted her onto his lap so she was straddling him. "They invited me over to your house for dinner tomorrow night. They want to get to know me before your father gives his full permission. It's understandable. I've also extended an invitation to them to visit my family in Australia." He smiled. "They seemed quite taken with that idea. By the way…" Alex gave her a serious look. "They don't know that you've been staying here with me at the hotel and I don't think we need to enlighten them."

She giggled, happiness and relief coursing through her. "No. What they don't know won't hurt them."

Alex kissed her then, taking her mouth and slanting his lips across hers then slipping his tongue into her mouth. Tanvi kissed him back, grasping his hair and pulling. He groaned and grasped her ass cheeks, squeezing and massaging.

He broke the kiss, breathing heavily. "I want you in the bedroom, naked and on your knees."

Tanvi's heart rate spiked, her pulse beating a frantic rhythm in her neck. "Yes, sir," she whispered. She climbed off his lap and scurried to the bedroom to do his bidding. She undressed quickly, unbraided her hair and knelt on the floor.

A moment later, Alex strode into the room. She looked at his feet as he undressed to his boxers.

He picked her up and flung her on the bed, the air whooshing out of her lungs. Then he swiftly tied her hands above her head to the bars and, grasping each of her ankles, he spread her legs wide, as wide as they'd go, the stretch pleasurably painful. He tied each leg to the bottom bars so she was in a starfish configuration. Her heart thrummed in her chest with nervous anticipation.

"I'm going to whip you with this," he murmured and held up a whip with thick, soft leather strands attached.

A shiver rippled through her, peaking her nipples to tight points.

Alex's pupils dilated, his gaze fixed on her breasts as he reached out to pinch her right nipple hard. She gasped and shivered, a pleasure-pain shooting from her nipples directly to her sex.

"What's your safe word, wife-to-be?"

"Kismet," she murmured, realizing that's exactly what this was. Her destiny, her future with Alex was the sweetest form of kismet.

About the Author

Jasmine was born in Australia and grew up in Sydney. She currently lives in Madrid, Spain with her husband.
She adores reading all genres but in particular she enjoys erotic romance novels and thrillers.

Jasmine loves writing and is always looking for new ideas for stories that will provoke inner passions, stimulate the senses and ignite the imagination.

Her interests include cooking, traveling, yoga and skiing. She has won some short story competitions and is now excited to have started publishing her erotic romance stories through Totally Bound Publishing.

Jasmine loves to hear from readers. You can find her contact information, website details and author profile page at http://www.totallybound.com.

TOTALLY
BOUND

Home of Erotic Romance